JAKE MADDOX
GRAPHIC NOVELS

WCMX
DAREDEVIL

MAR 1 6 2022

STONE ARCH BOOKS
a capstone imprint

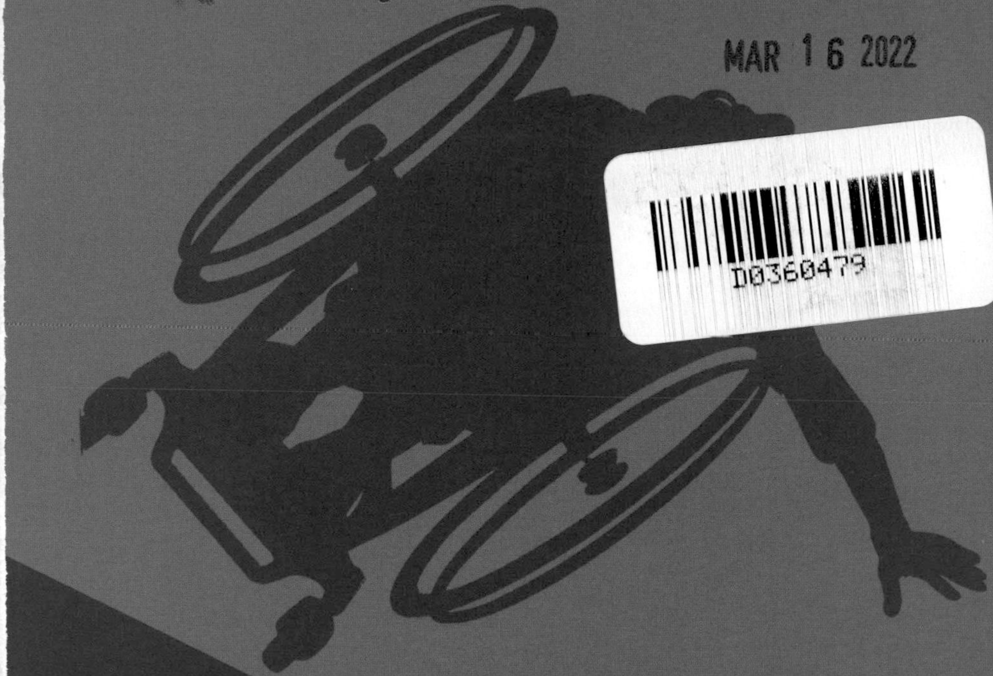

JAKE MADDOX
GRAPHIC NOVELS

Published by Stone Arch Books,
an imprint of Capstone.
1710 Roe Crest Drive
North Mankato, Minnesota 56003
capstonepub.com

Library in Congress Cataloging-in-Publication Data
Names: Maddox, Jake, author. | Pryor, Shawn, author. | Vitrano, Erika, illustrator.
Title: WCMX daredevil / Jake Maddox ; text by Shawn Pryor ; [illustrator Erika Vitrano].
Other titles: Jake Maddox graphic novels.
Description: North Mankato, Minnesota : Stone Arch Books, an imprint of Capstone, [2022] | Series: Jake Maddox graphic novels | Audience: Ages 8-11. | Audience: Grades 2-3.
Summary: Davalyn Hart was born with spina bifida, but she is determined not to let that define her, and, being a daredevil, she has taken up the sport of wheelchair motocross; now that she has a brand new, specially designed wheelchair, she is ready to fly--until a bad fall while trying to impress another player shakes her confidence.
Identifiers: LCCN 2021030690 (print) | LCCN 2021030691 (ebook) | ISBN 9781663959164 (hardcover) | ISBN 9781666328646 (paperback) | ISBN 9781666328653 (pdf) | ISBN 9781666328677 (kindle edition) Subjects: LCSH: Wheelchair sports--Comic books, strips, etc. | Wheelchair sports--Juvenile fiction. | African American girls-- Comic books, strips, etc. | African American girls--Juvenile fiction. | Spina bifida--Comic books, strips, etc. | Spina bifida--Juvenile fiction. | Self-confidence--Comic books, strips, etc. | Self-confidence--Juvenile fiction. | CYAC: Motocross--Fiction. | Wheelchairs--Fiction. | Spina bifida-- Fiction. | People with disabilities--Fiction. | Self-confidence--Fiction. | African Americans--Fiction.
Classification: LCC PZ7.7.M332 Wc 2022 (print) | LCC PZ7.7.M332 (ebook) | DDC 741.5/973--dc23
LC record available at https:// lccn.loc.gov/2021030690
LC ebook record available at https://lccn.loc.gov/ 2021030691

Editor: Aaron Sautter
Designer: Brann Garvey
Production Specialist: Laura Manthe

Printed and bound in the USA. PO4608

WCMX DAREDEVIL

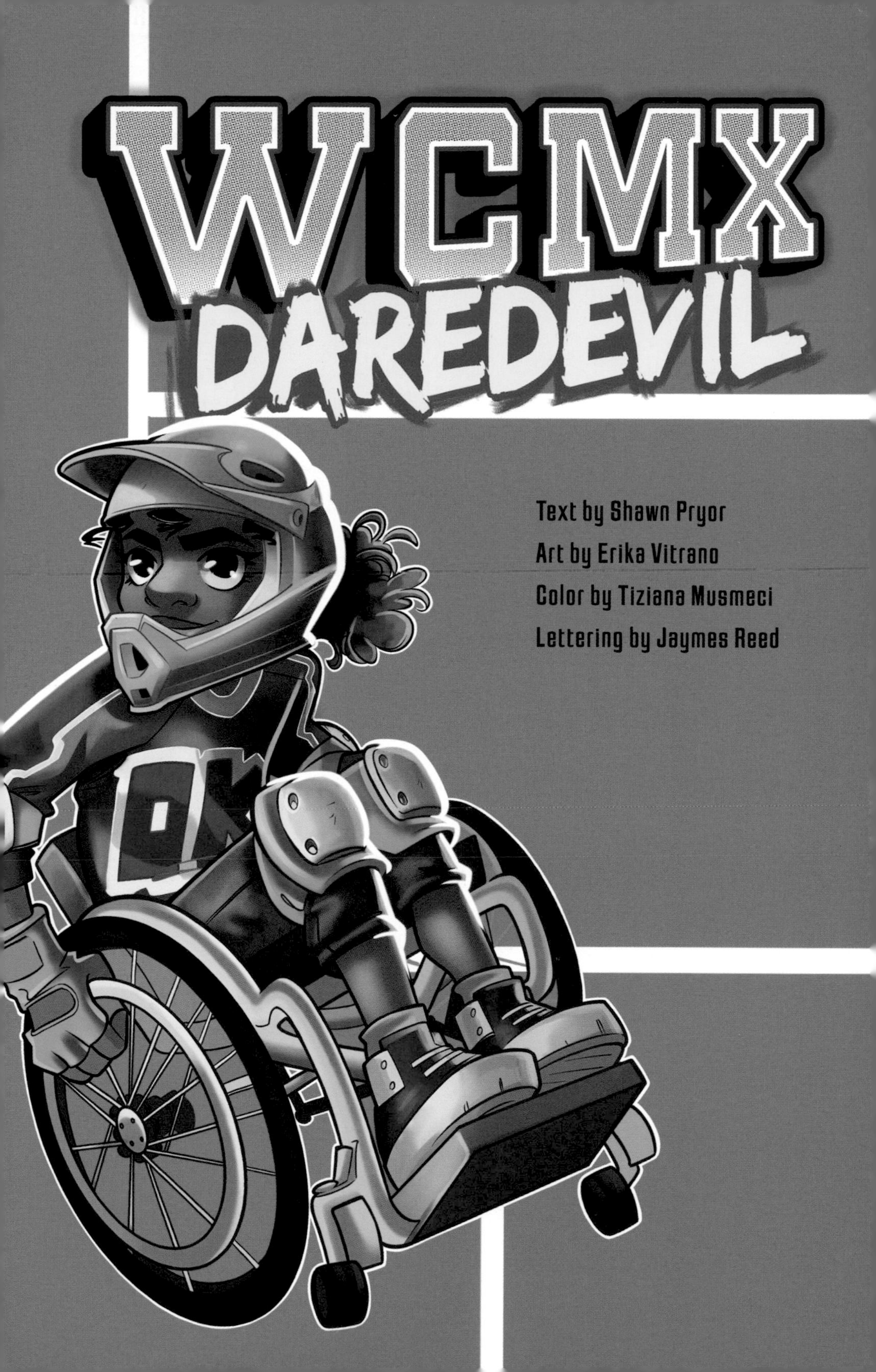

Text by Shawn Pryor
Art by Erika Vitrano
Color by Tiziana Musmeci
Lettering by Jaymes Reed

CAST OF CHARACTERS

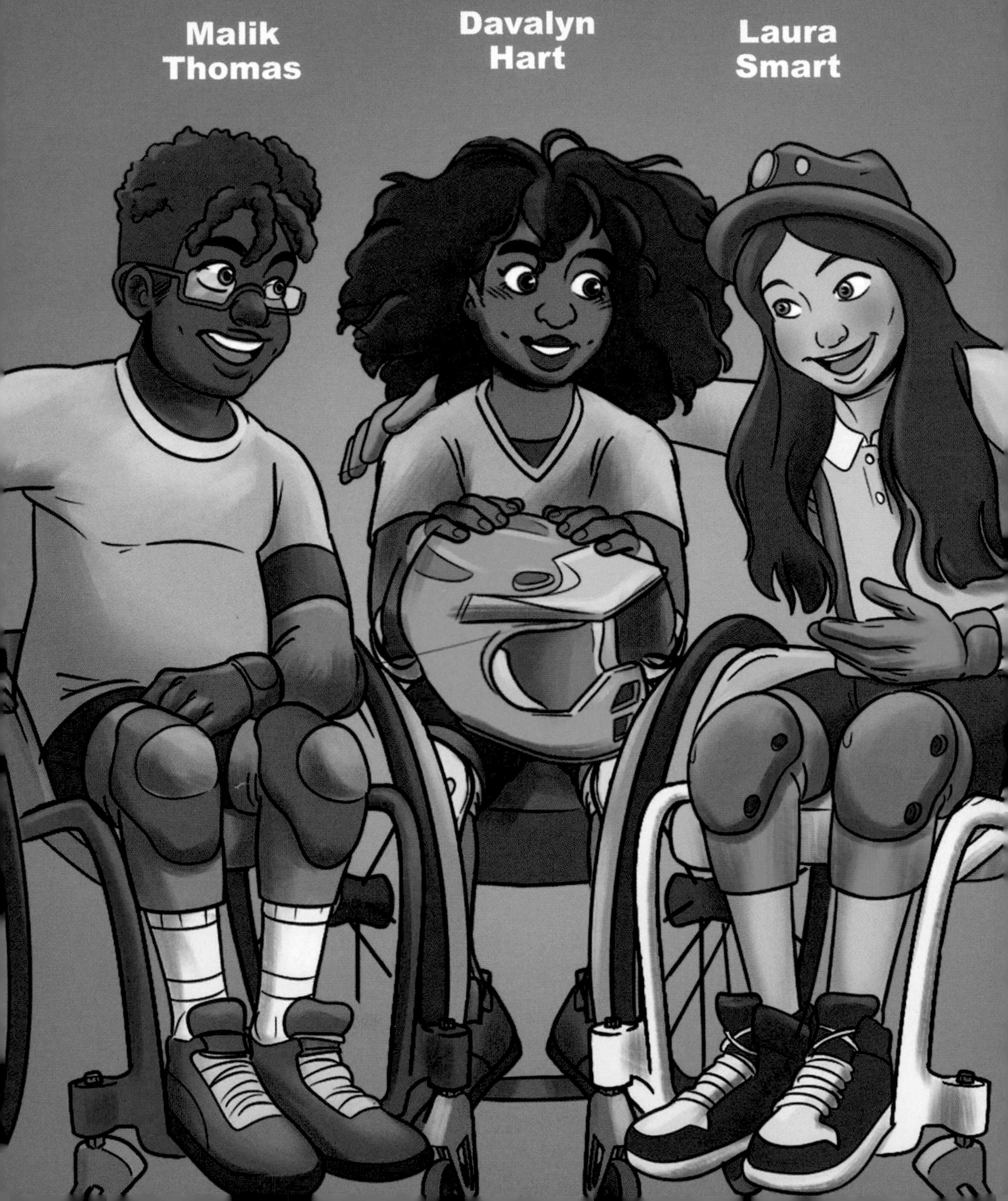
Malik Thomas
Davalyn Hart
Laura Smart

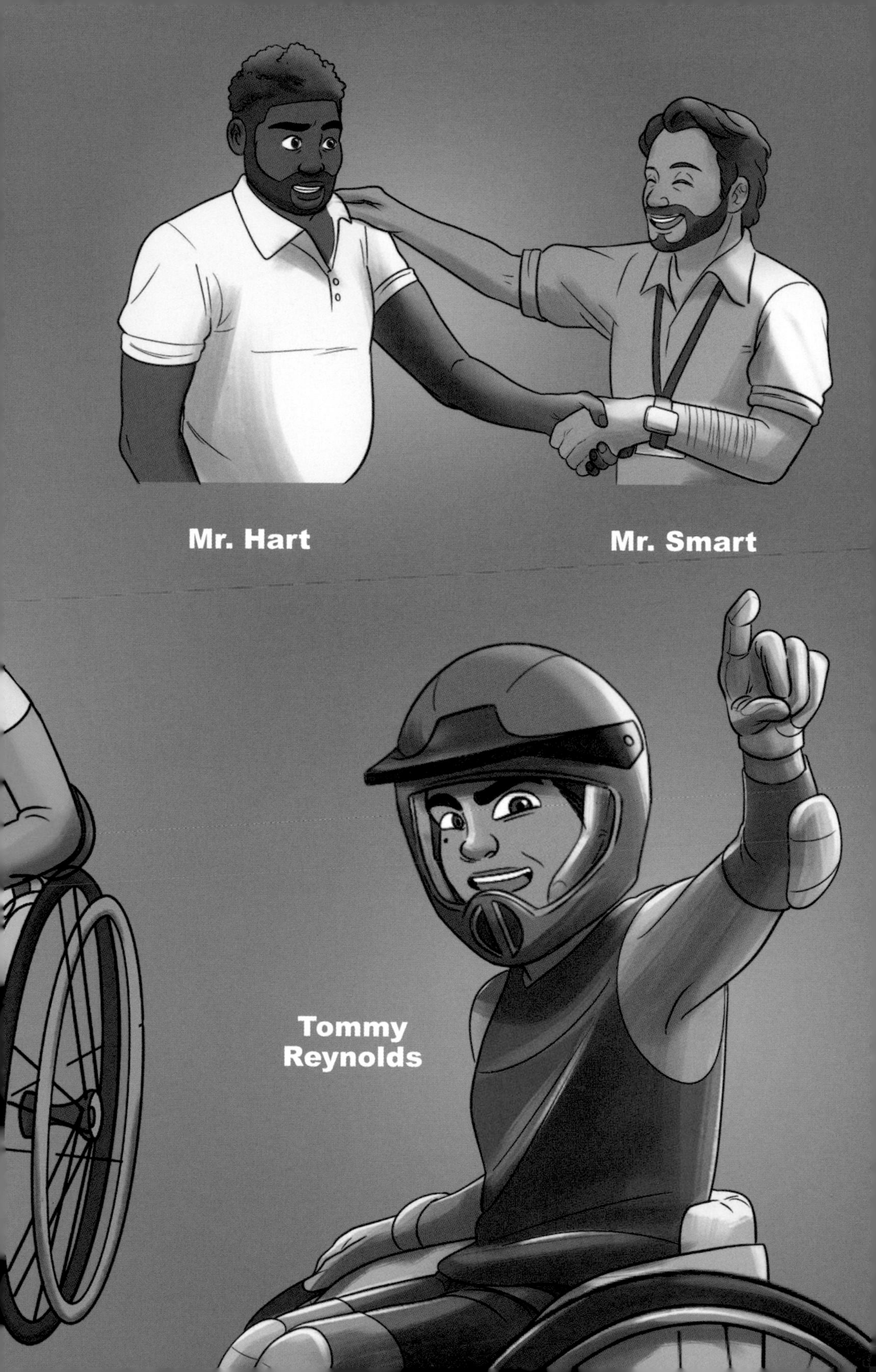
Mr. Hart
Mr. Smart
Tommy Reynolds

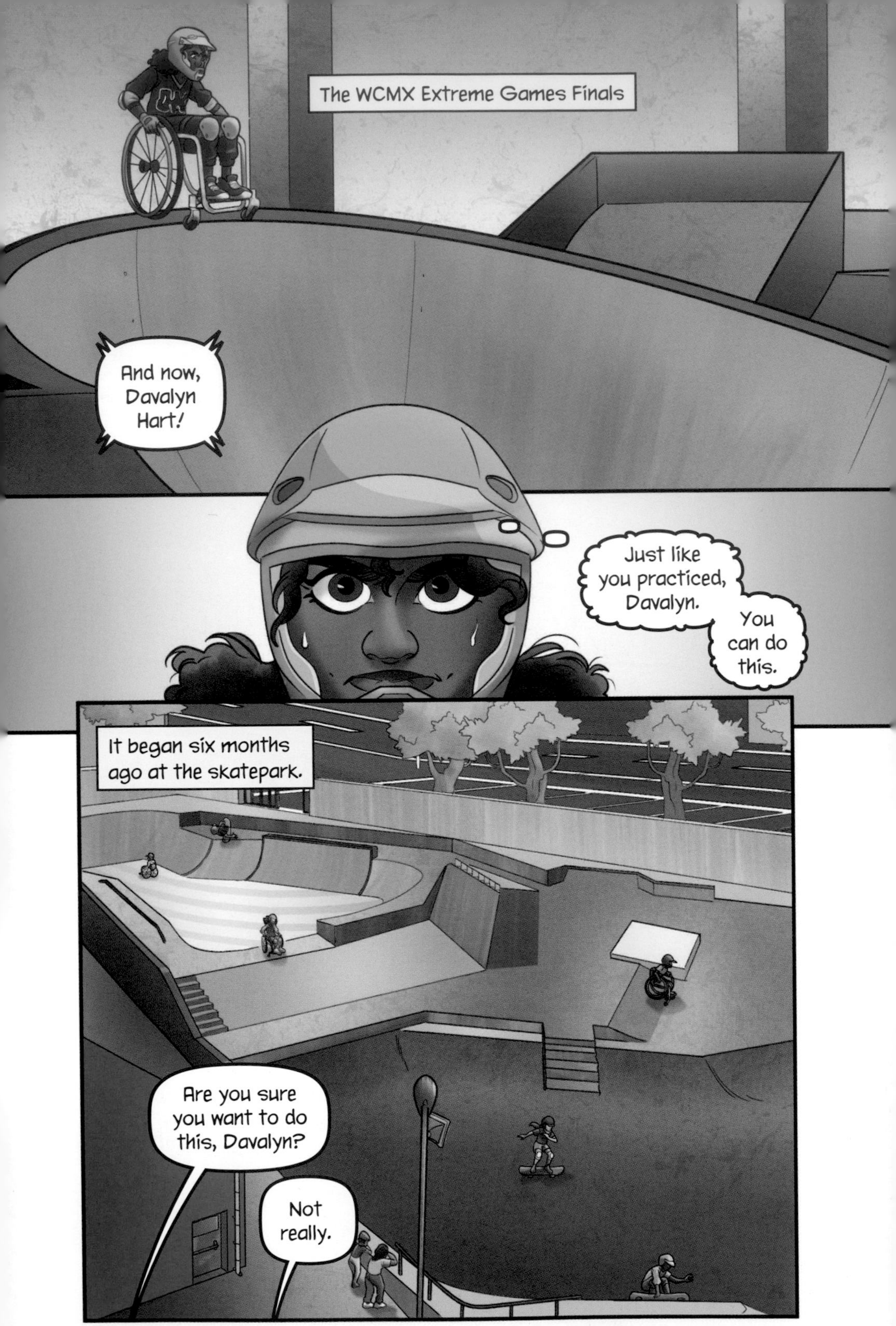

The WCMX Extreme Games Finals
And now, Davalyn Hart!
Just like you practiced, Davalyn.
You can do this.
It began six months ago at the skatepark.
Are you sure you want to do this, Davalyn?
Not really.

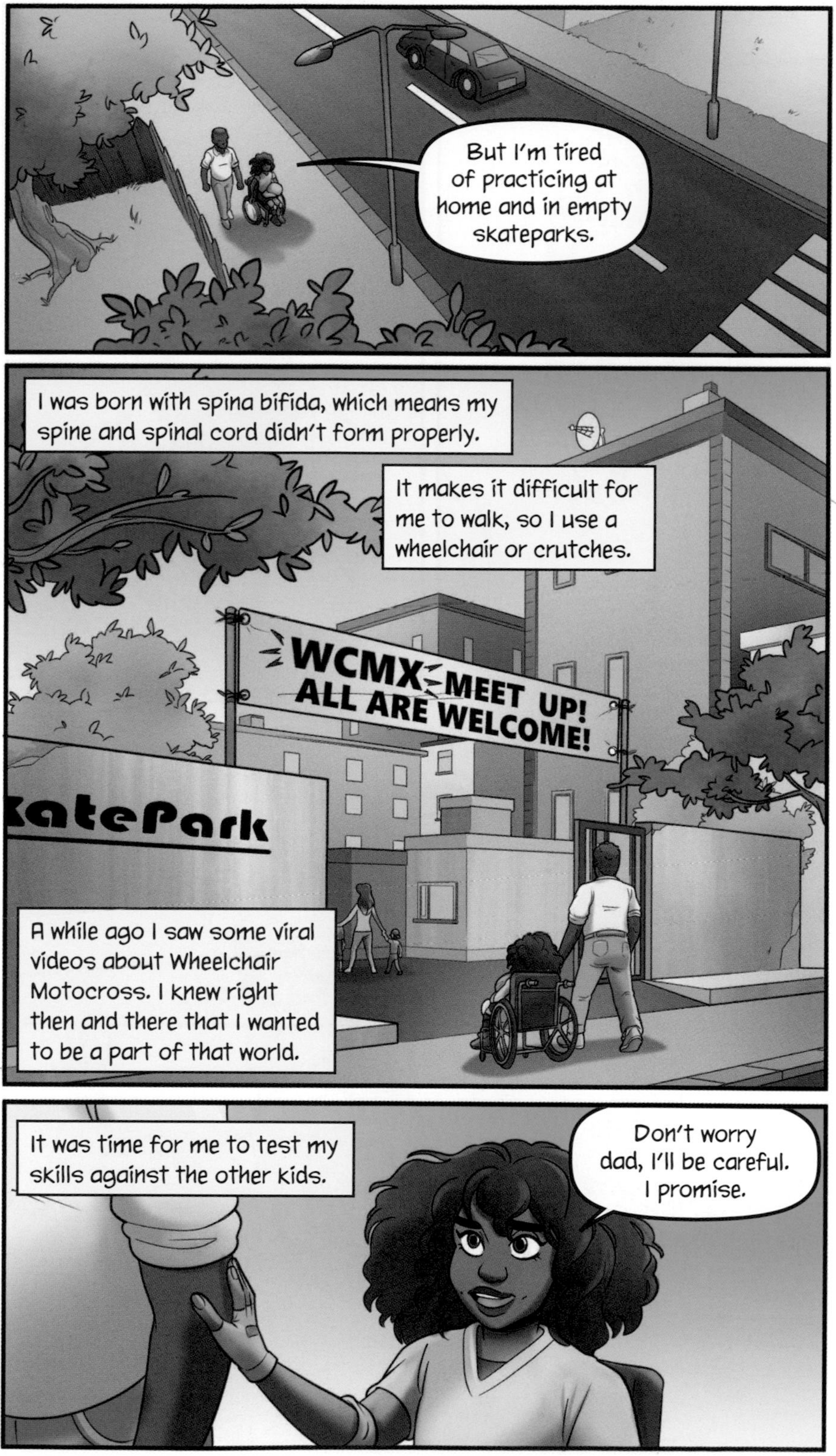
But I'm tired of practicing at home and in empty skateparks.
I was born with spina bifida, which means my spine and spinal cord didn't form properly.
It makes it difficult for me to walk, so I use a wheelchair or crutches.
WCMX MEET UP! ALL ARE WELCOME!
katePark
A while ago I saw some viral videos about Wheelchair Motocross. I knew right then and there that I wanted to be a part of that world.
It was time for me to test my skills against the other kids.
Don't worry dad, I'll be careful. I promise.

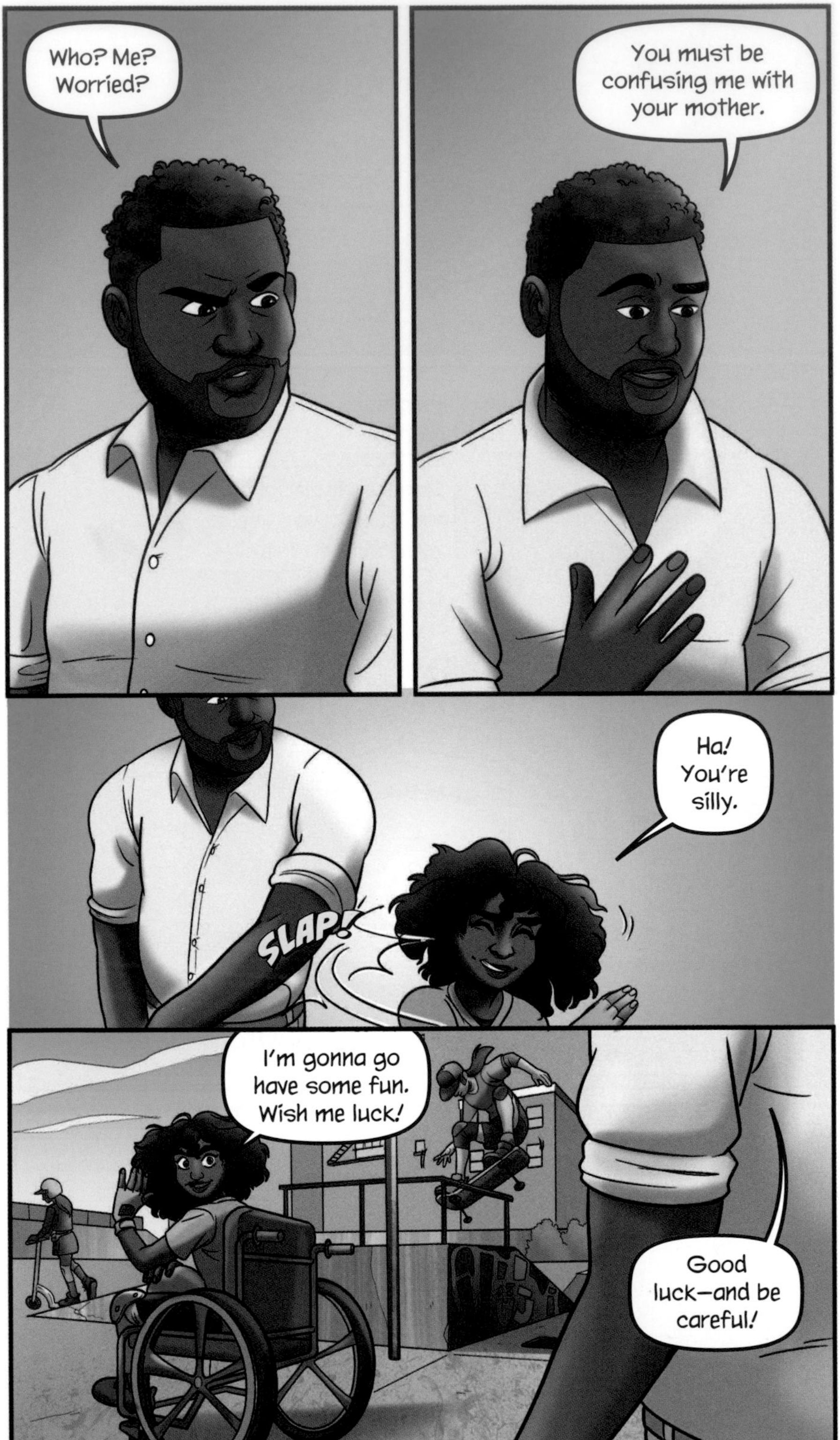
Who? Me? Worried?
You must be confusing me with your mother.
SLAP!
Ha! You're silly.
I'm gonna go have some fun. Wish me luck!
Good luck—and be careful!

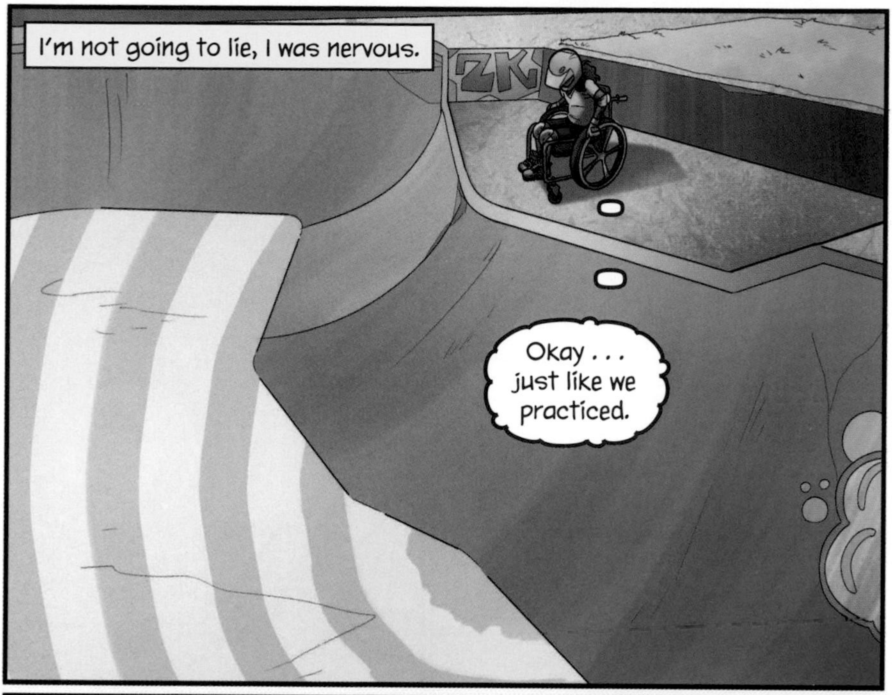
I'm not going to lie, I was nervous.
Okay . . . just like we practiced.

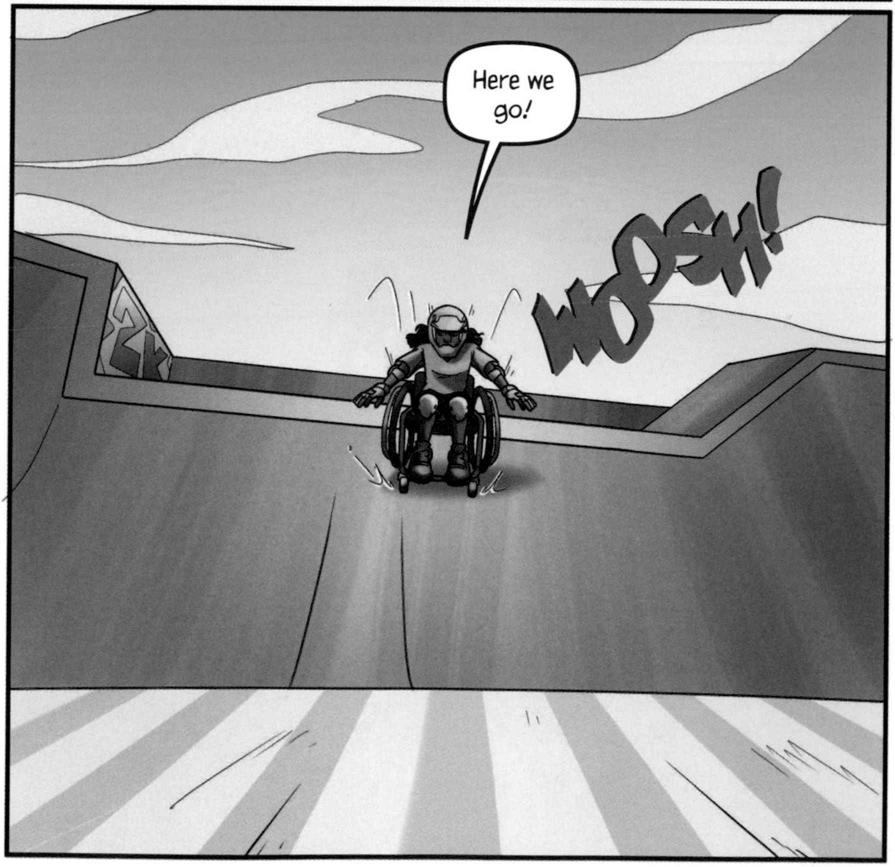
Here we go!
WOOSH!

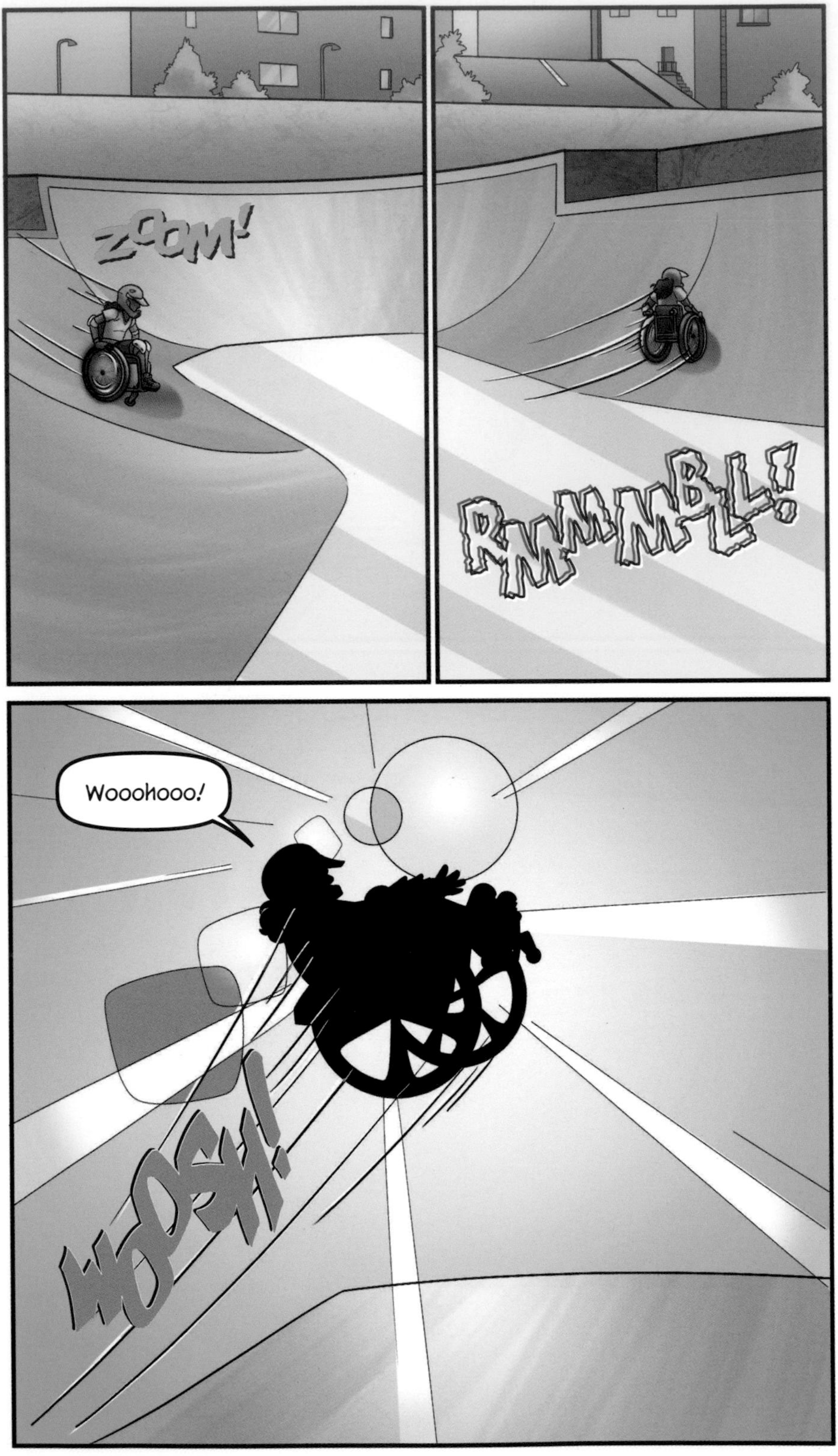
ZOOM!
RMMMBLL!
Wooohooo!
WOOSH!

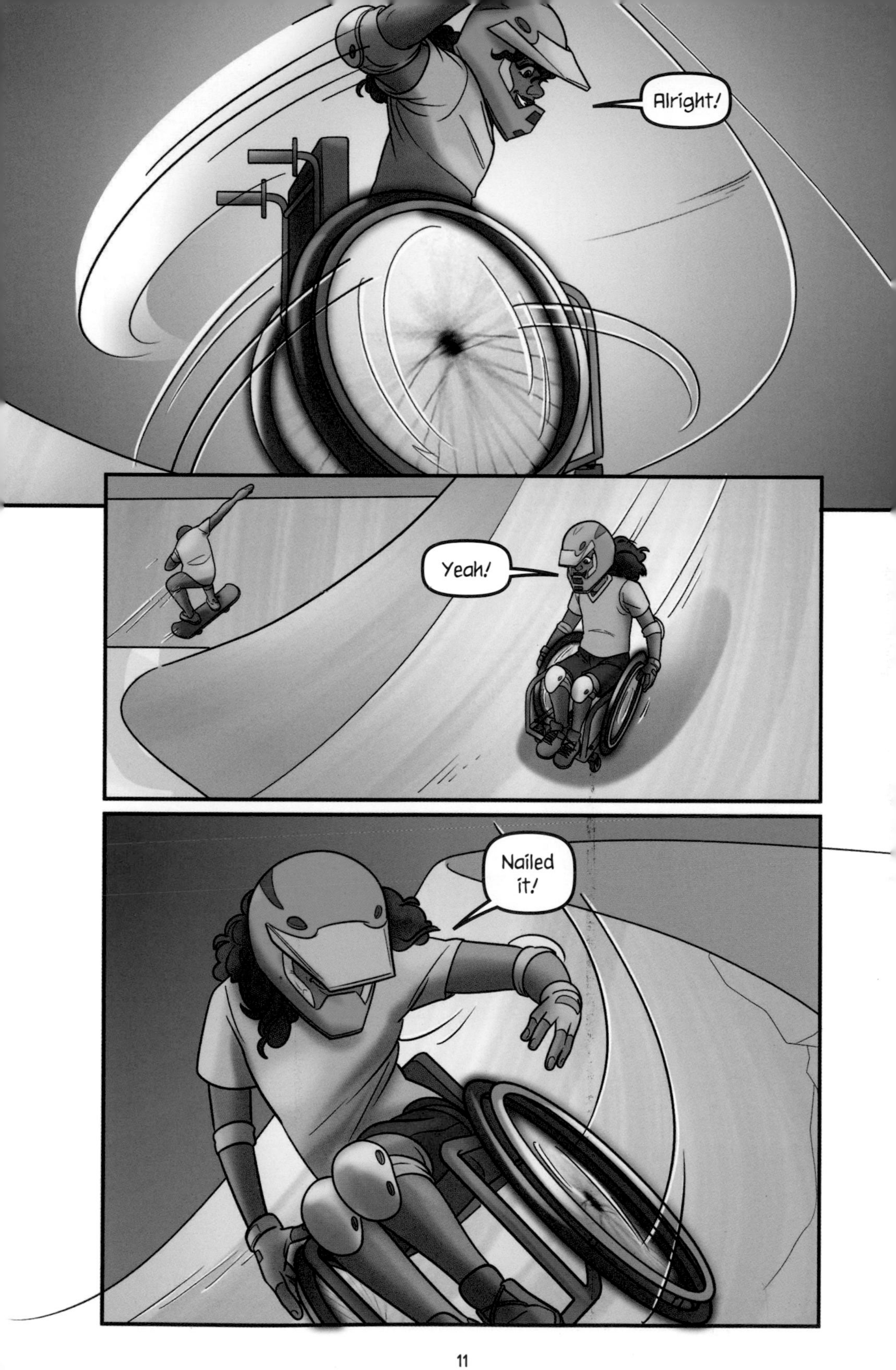
Alright!
Yeah!
Nailed it!

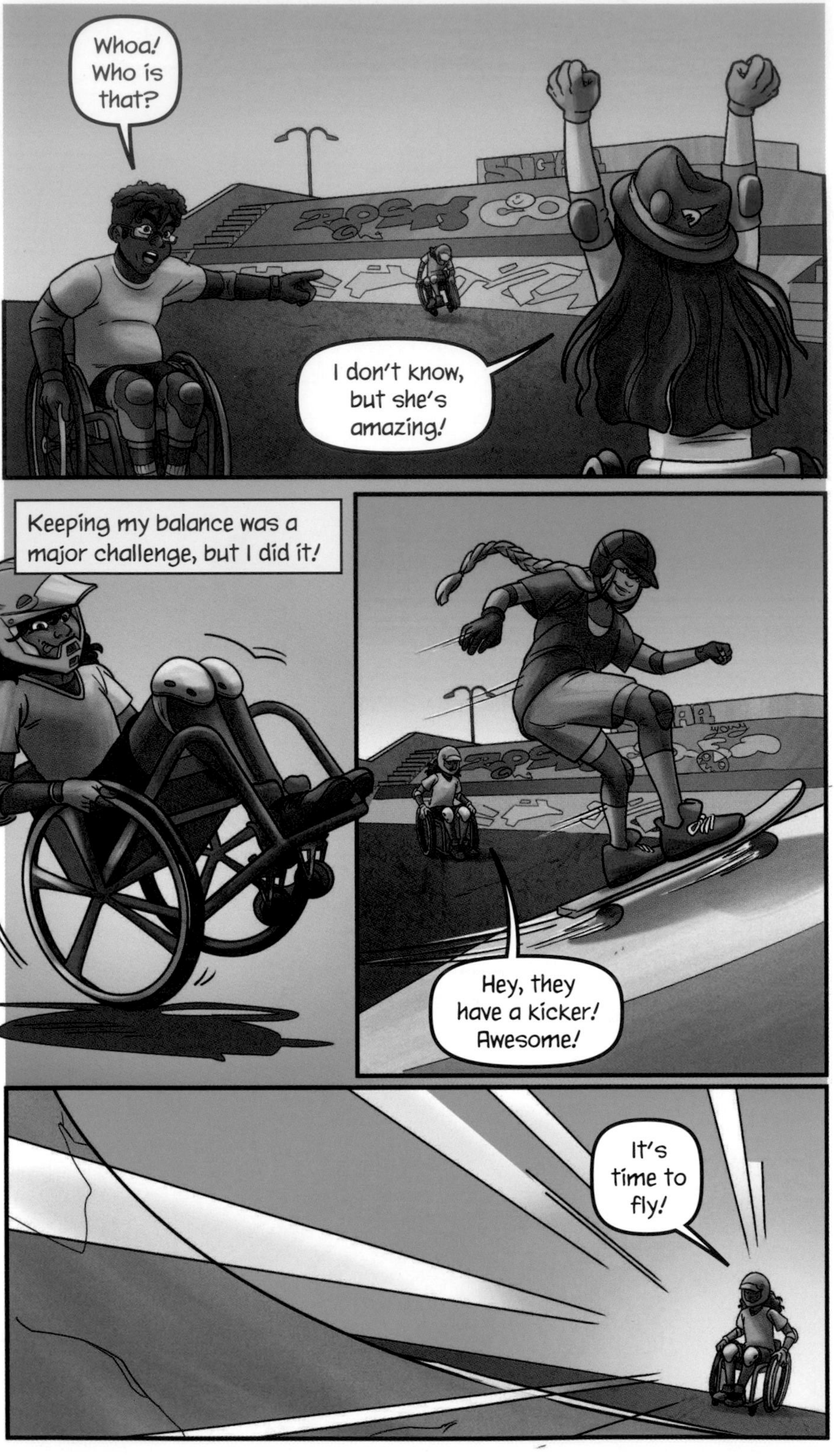
Whoa! Who is that?
I don't know, but she's amazing!
Keeping my balance was a major challenge, but I did it!
Hey, they have a kicker! Awesome!
It's time to fly!

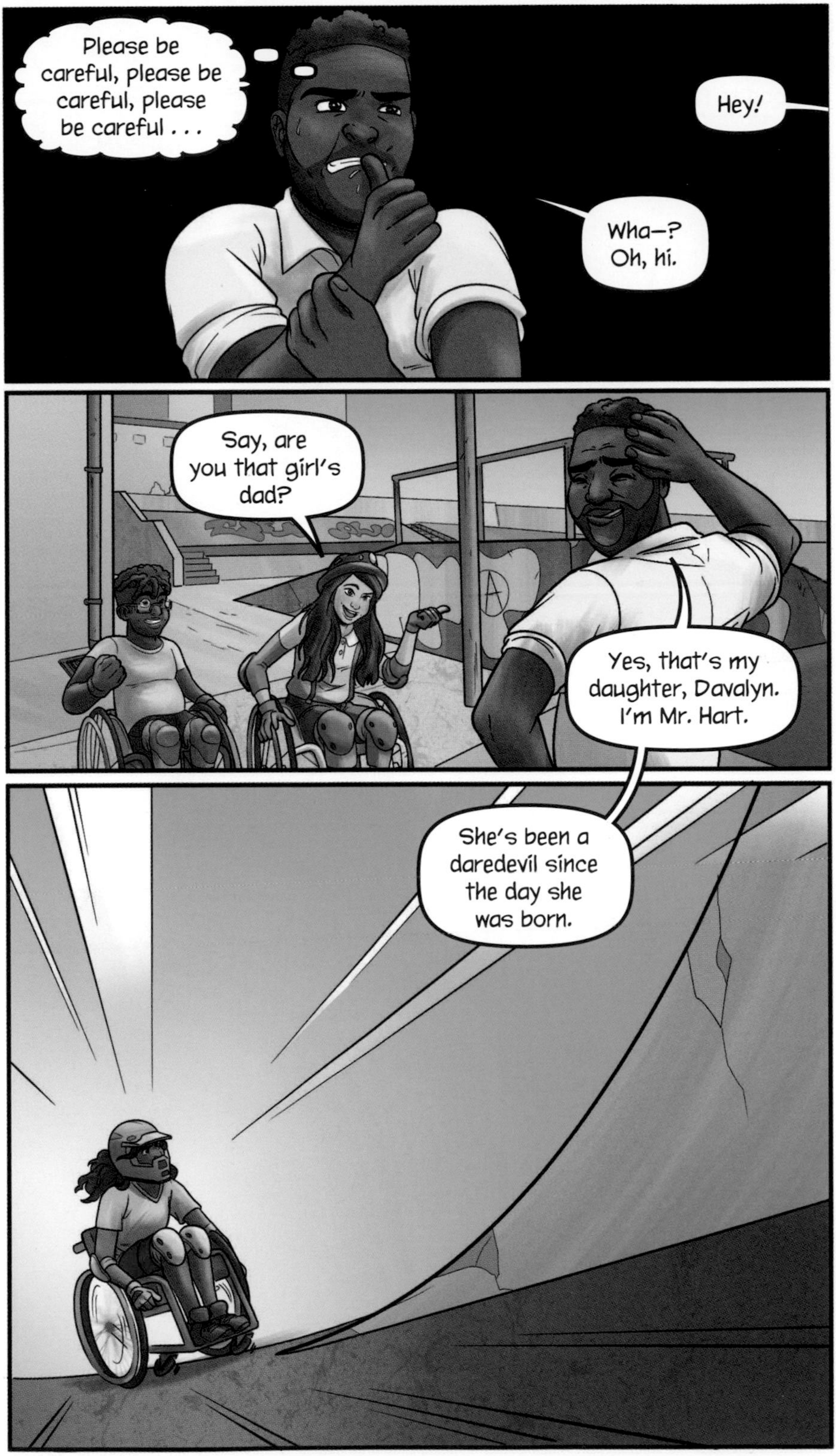
Please be careful, please be careful, please be careful . . .
Hey!
Wha—? Oh, hi.
Say, are you that girl's dad?
Yes, that's my daughter, Davalyn. I'm Mr. Hart.
She's been a daredevil since the day she was born.

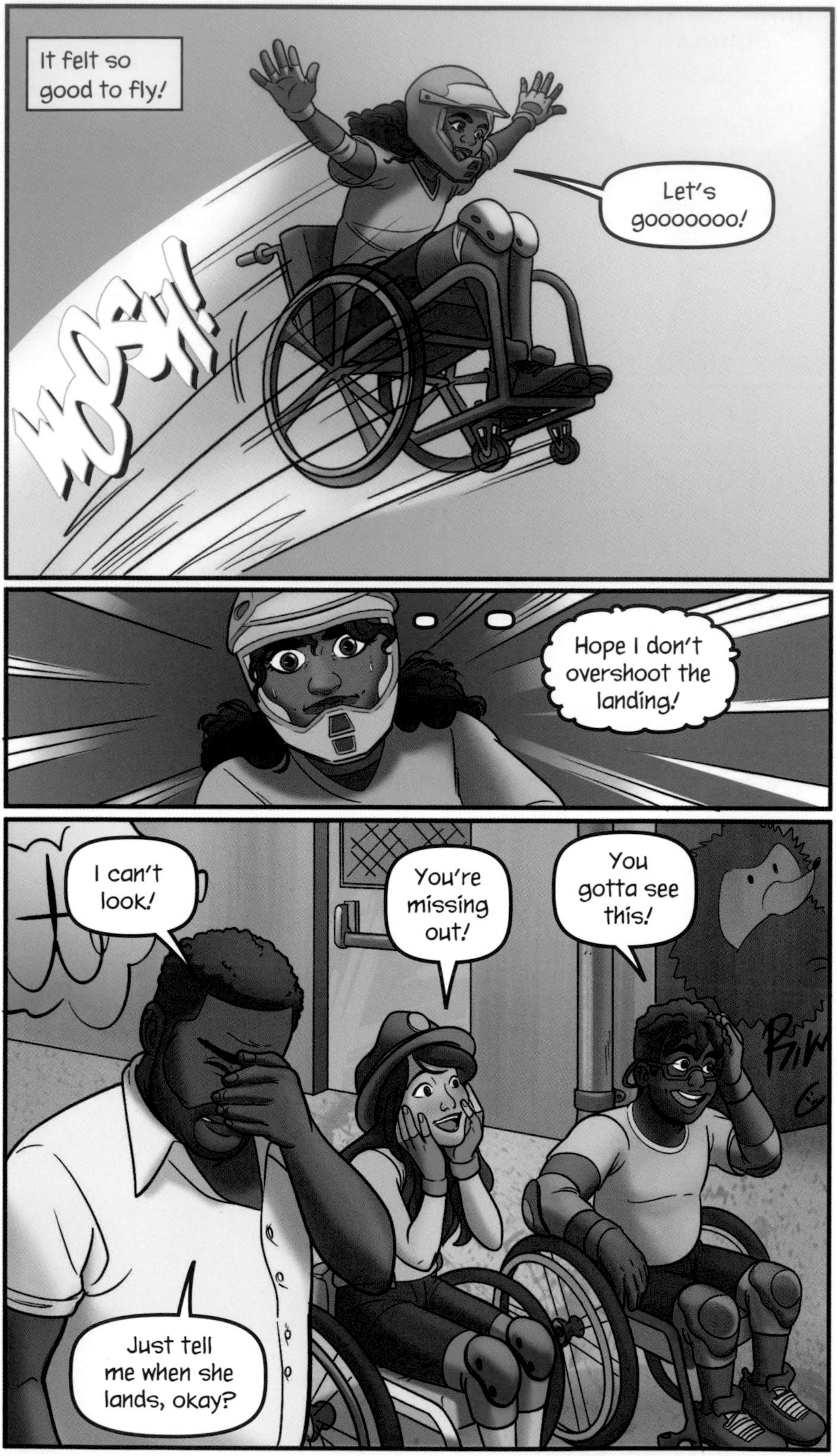
It felt so good to fly!
Let's goooooooo!
WHOOSH!
Hope I don't overshoot the landing!
I can't look!
You're missing out!
You gotta see this!
Just tell me when she lands, okay?

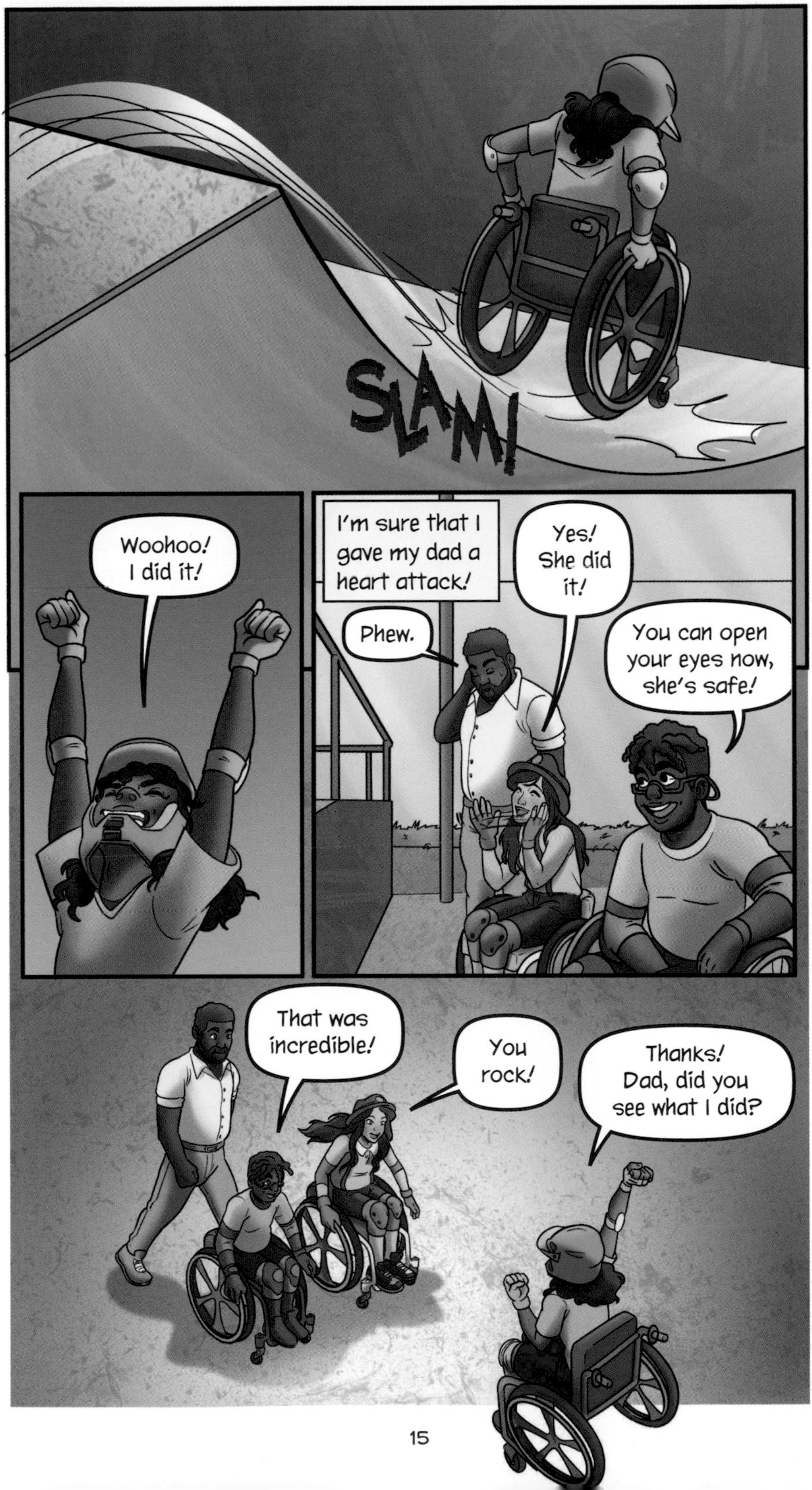
SLAM!
Woohoo! I did it!
I'm sure that I gave my dad a heart attack!
Phew.
Yes! She did it!
You can open your eyes now, she's safe!
That was incredible!
You rock!
Thanks! Dad, did you see what I did?

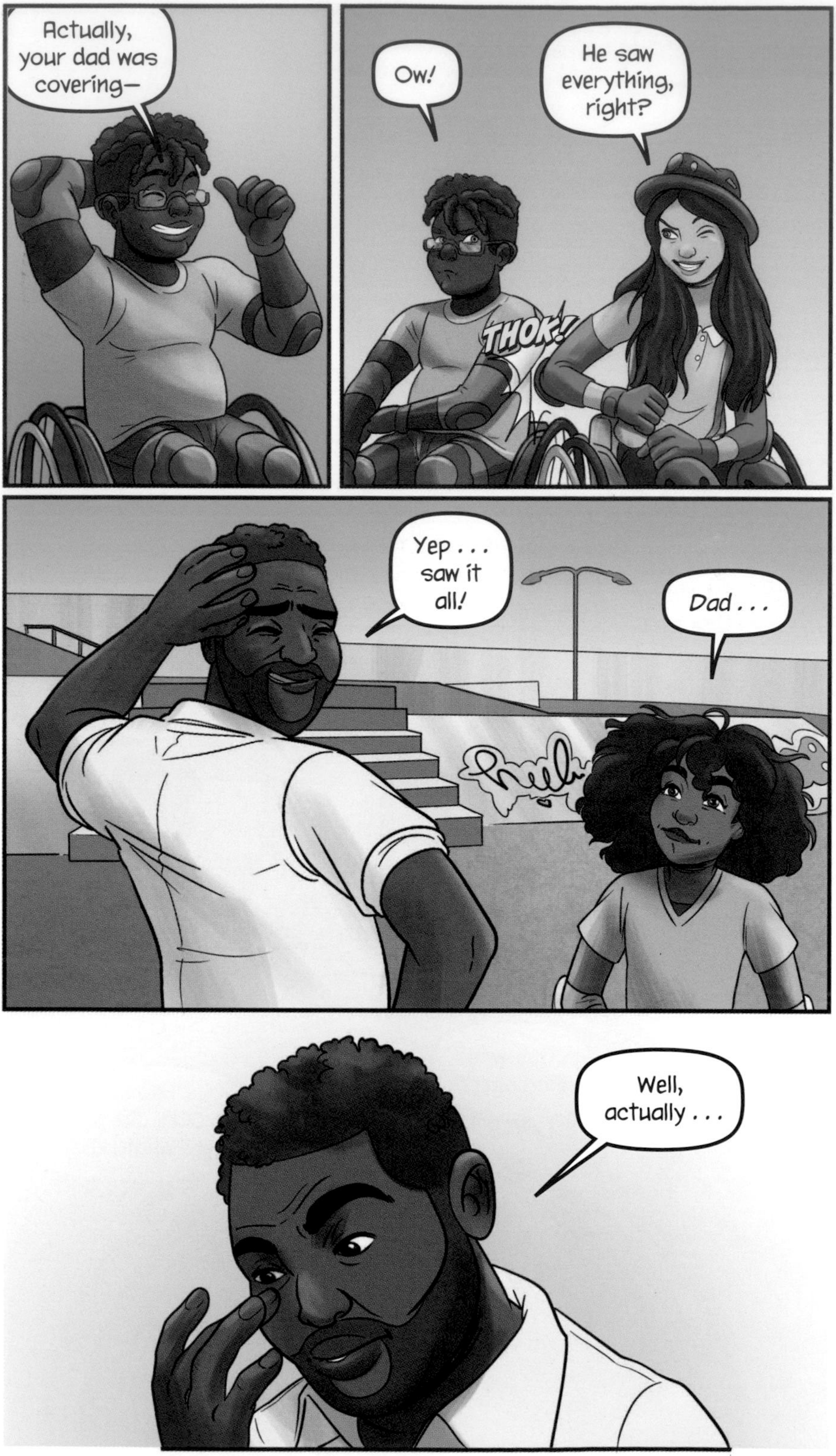
Actually, your dad was covering—
Ow!
THOK!
He saw everything, right?
Yep . . . saw it all!
Dad . . .
Well, actually . . .

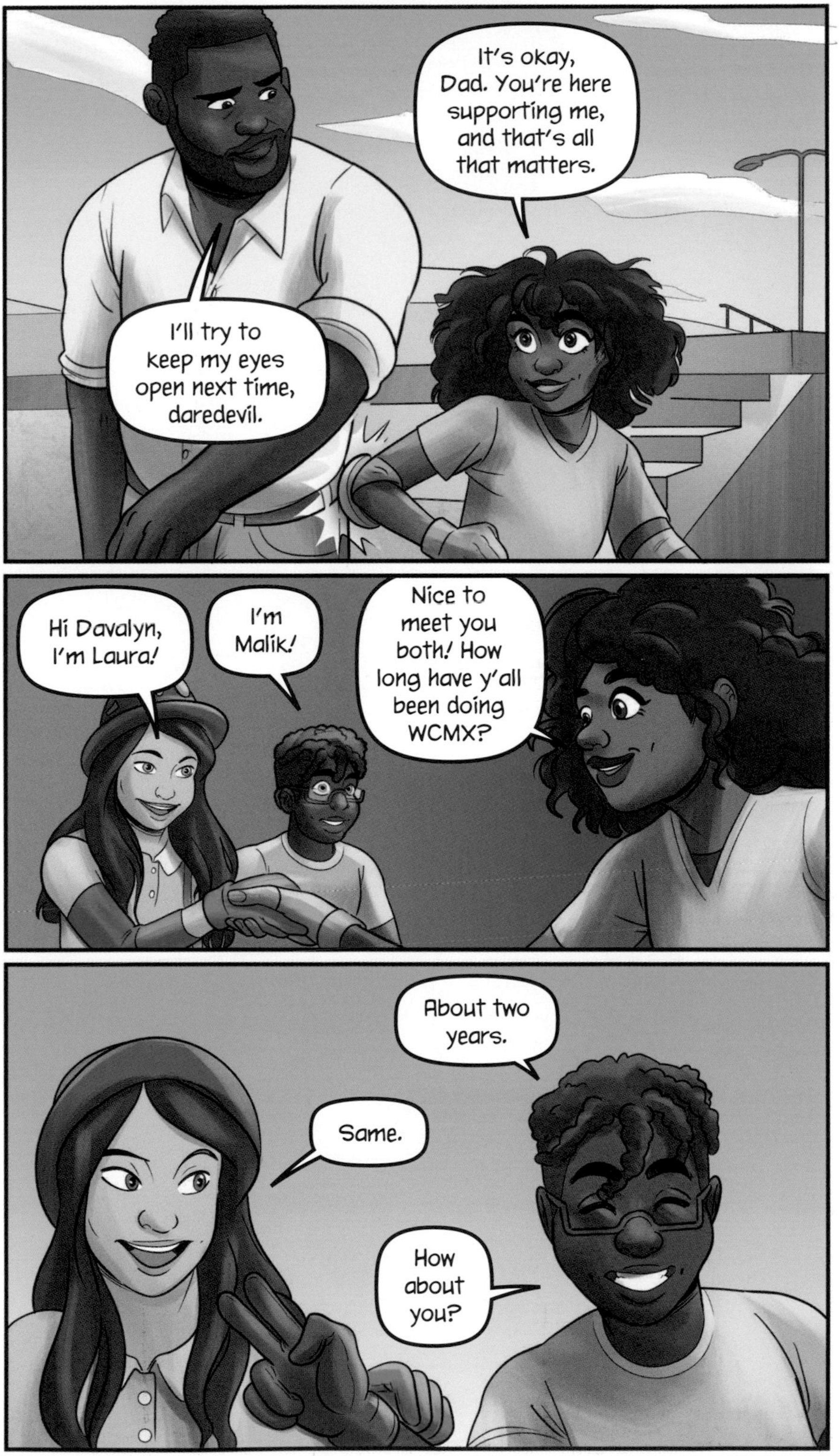
It's okay, Dad. You're here supporting me, and that's all that matters.
I'll try to keep my eyes open next time, daredevil.
Hi Davalyn, I'm Laura!
I'm Malik!
Nice to meet you both! How long have y'all been doing WCMX?
About two years.
Same.
How about you?

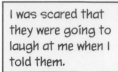
I was scared that they were going to laugh at me when I told them.

Um, well . . . three months?

Seriously?!

Is that a bad thing?

But their reaction was totally cool. I was so relieved!

Are you kidding? That's not bad at all!

Who taught you your moves?

Some of the things you did today, I'm still learning how to do!

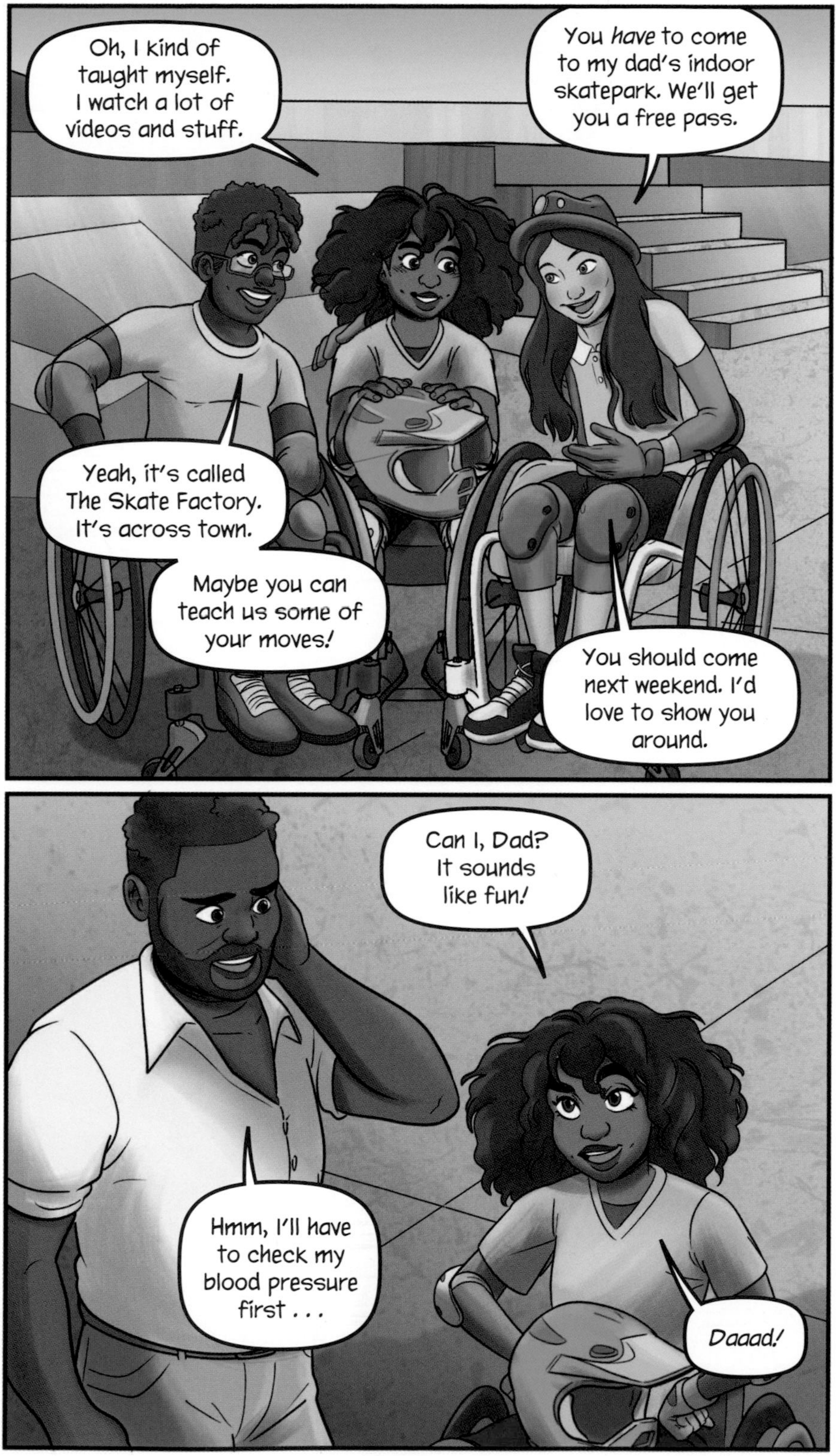
Oh, I kind of taught myself. I watch a lot of videos and stuff.
You *have* to come to my dad's indoor skatepark. We'll get you a free pass.
Yeah, it's called The Skate Factory. It's across town.
Maybe you can teach us some of your moves!
You should come next weekend. I'd love to show you around.
Can I, Dad? It sounds like fun!
Hmm, I'll have to check my blood pressure first . . .
Daaad!

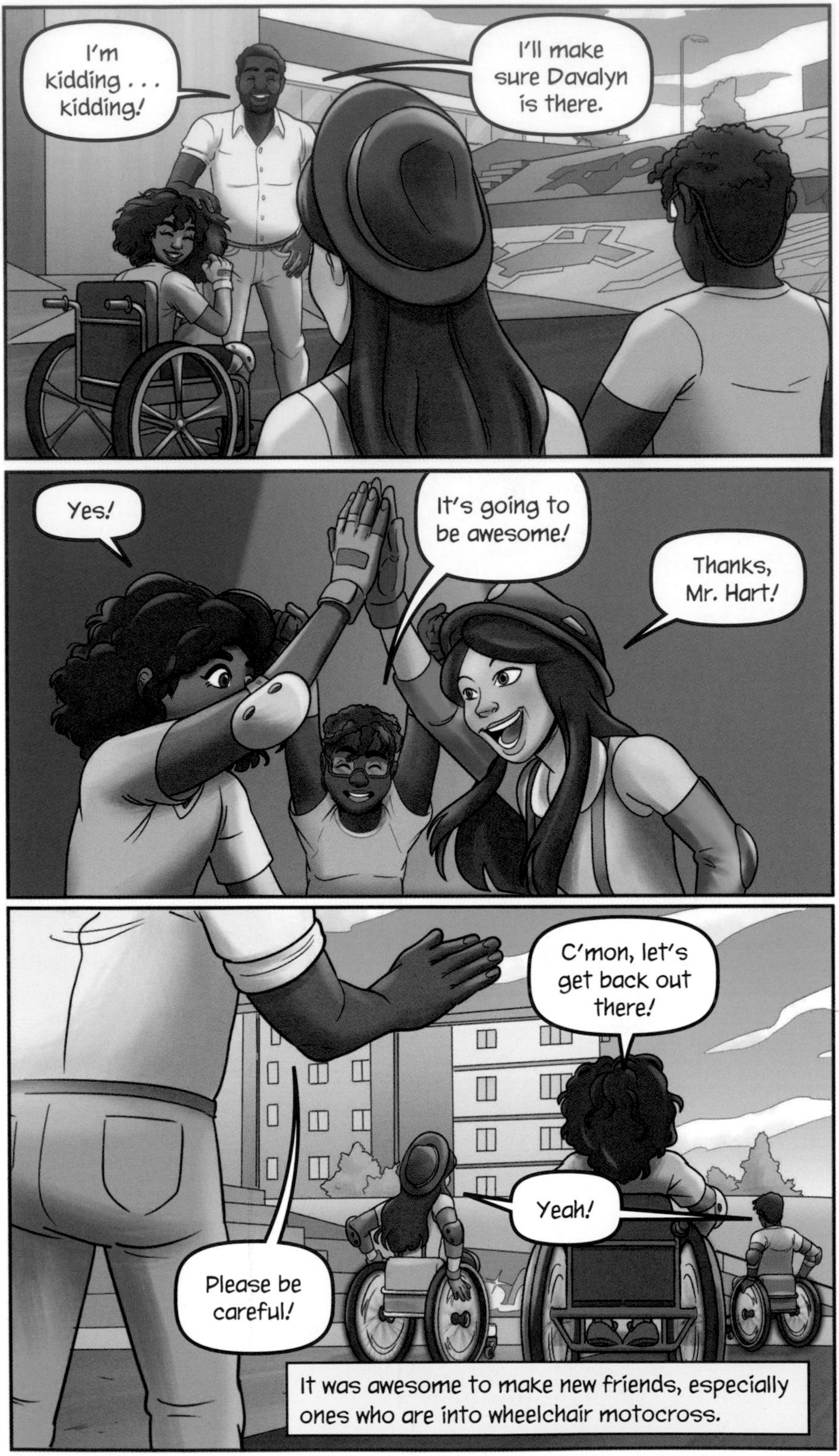
I'm kidding . . . kidding!
I'll make sure Davalyn is there.
Yes!
It's going to be awesome!
Thanks, Mr. Hart!
C'mon, let's get back out there!
Yeah!
Please be careful!
It was awesome to make new friends, especially ones who are into wheelchair motocross.

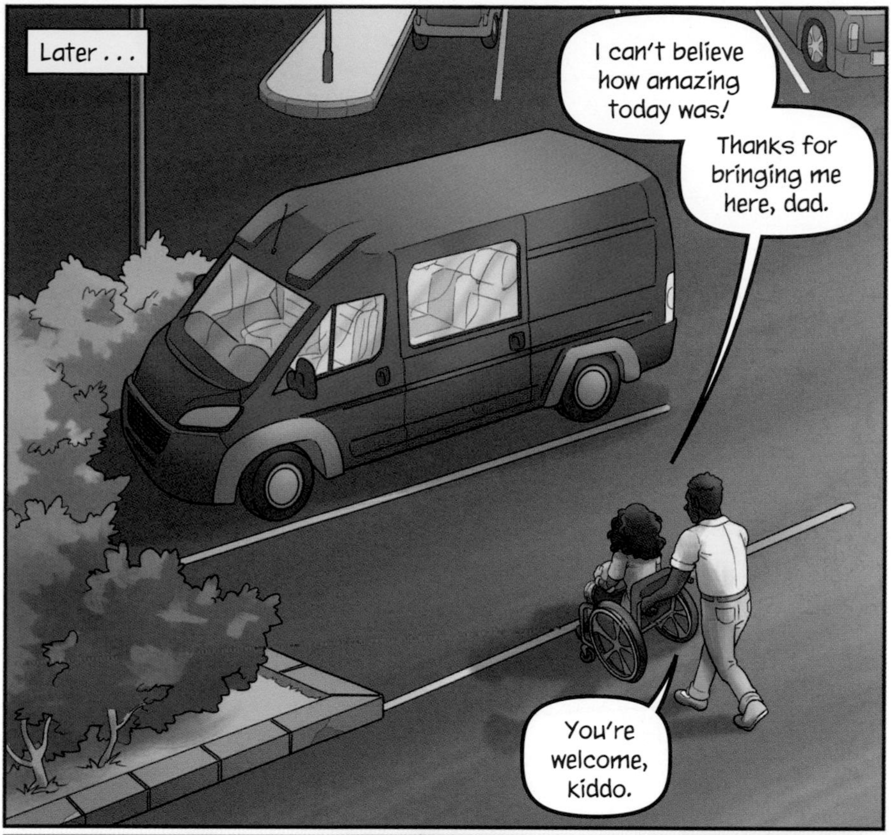
Later . . .
I can't believe how amazing today was!
Thanks for bringing me here, dad.
You're welcome, kiddo.

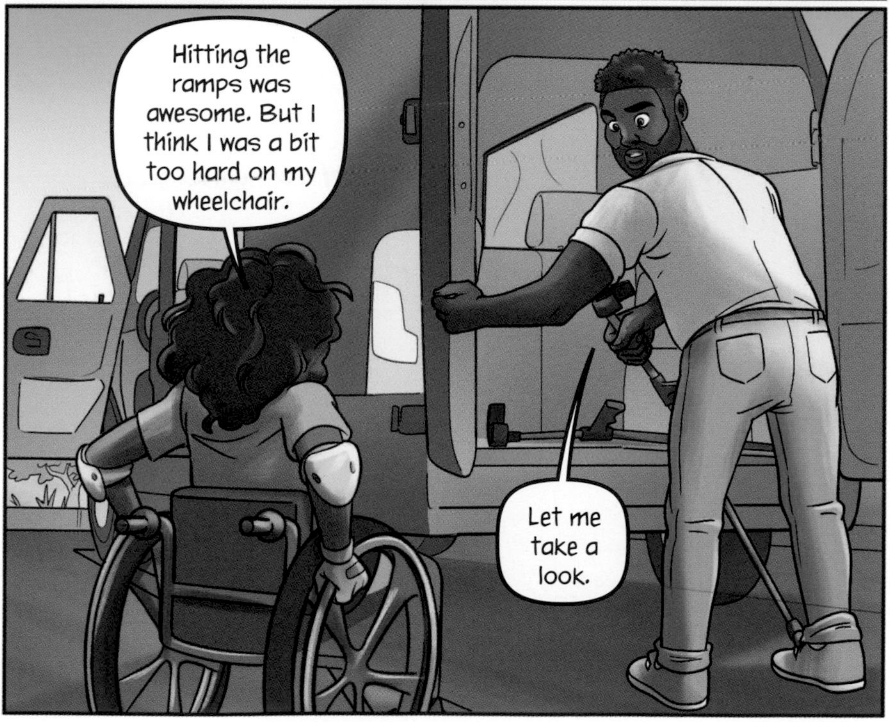
Hitting the ramps was awesome. But I think I was a bit too hard on my wheelchair.
Let me take a look.

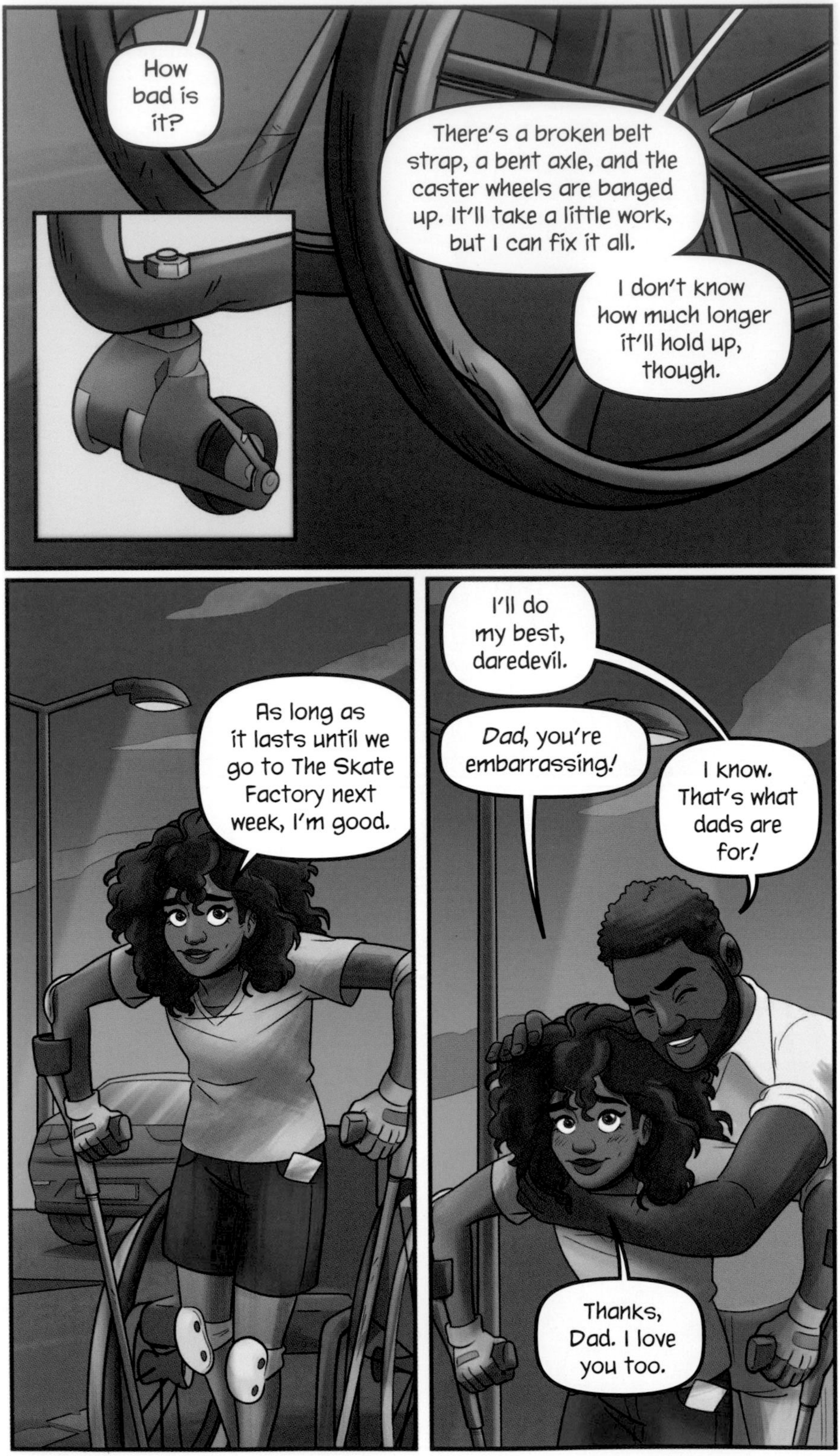
How bad is it?
There's a broken belt strap, a bent axle, and the caster wheels are banged up. It'll take a little work, but I can fix it all.
I don't know how much longer it'll hold up, though.
As long as it lasts until we go to The Skate Factory next week, I'm good.
I'll do my best, daredevil.
Dad, you're embarrassing!
I know. That's what dads are for!
Thanks, Dad. I love you too.

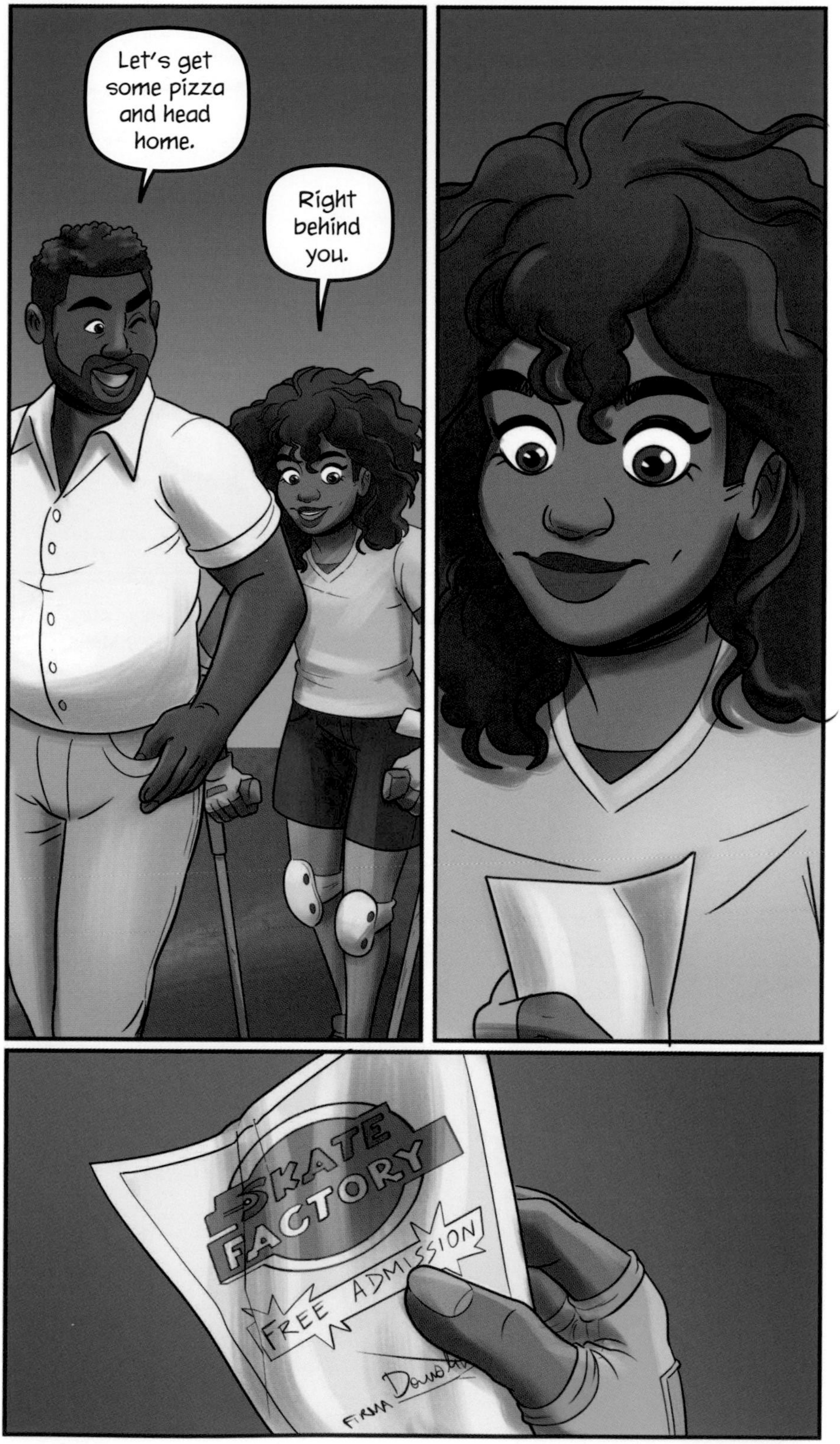
Let's get some pizza and head home.
Right behind you.
SKATE FACTORY
FREE ADMISSION

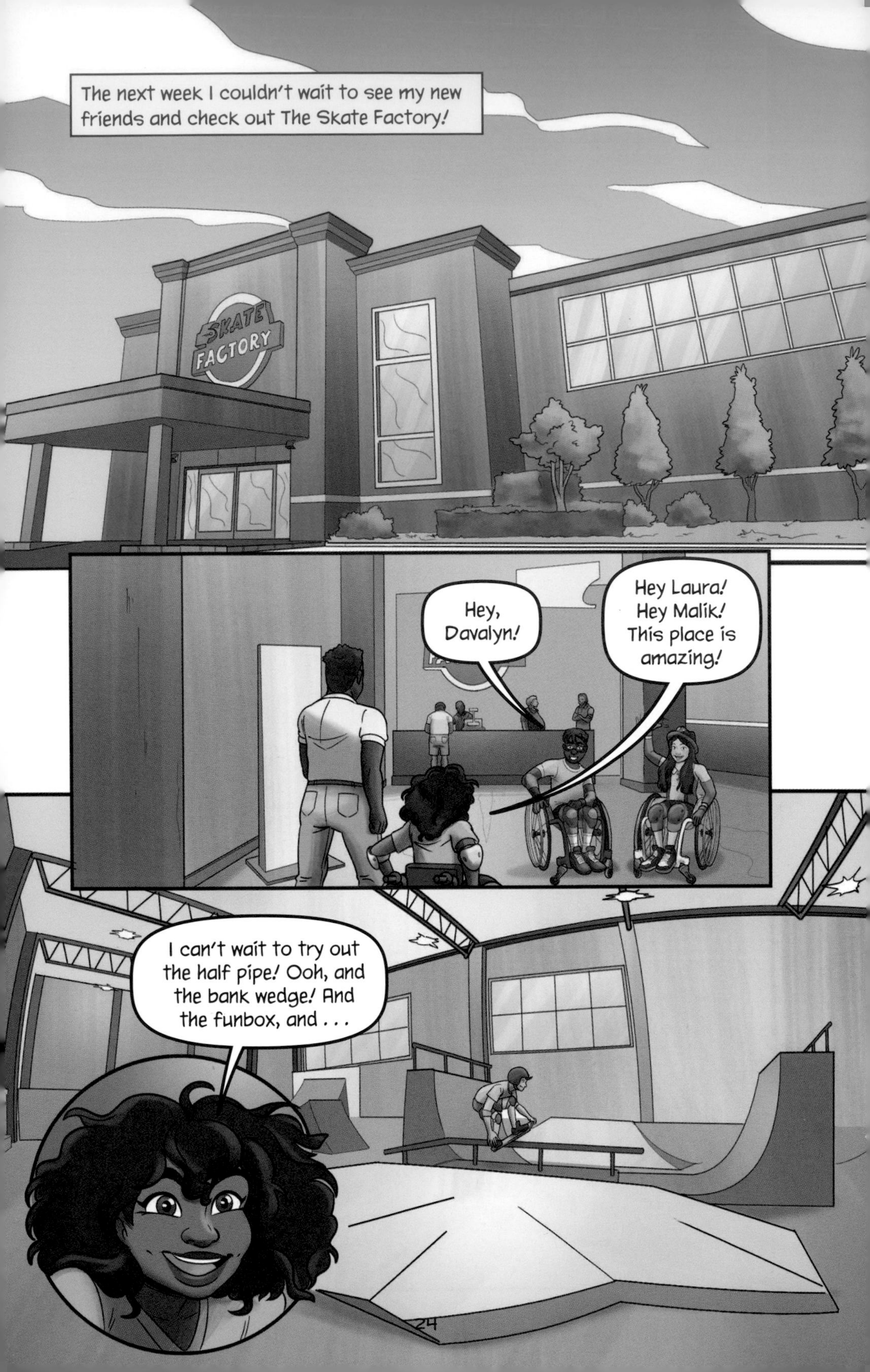
The next week I couldn't wait to see my new friends and check out The Skate Factory!
SKATE FACTORY
Hey, Davalyn!
Hey Laura! Hey Malik! This place is amazing!
I can't wait to try out the half pipe! Ooh, and the bank wedge! And the funbox, and . . .

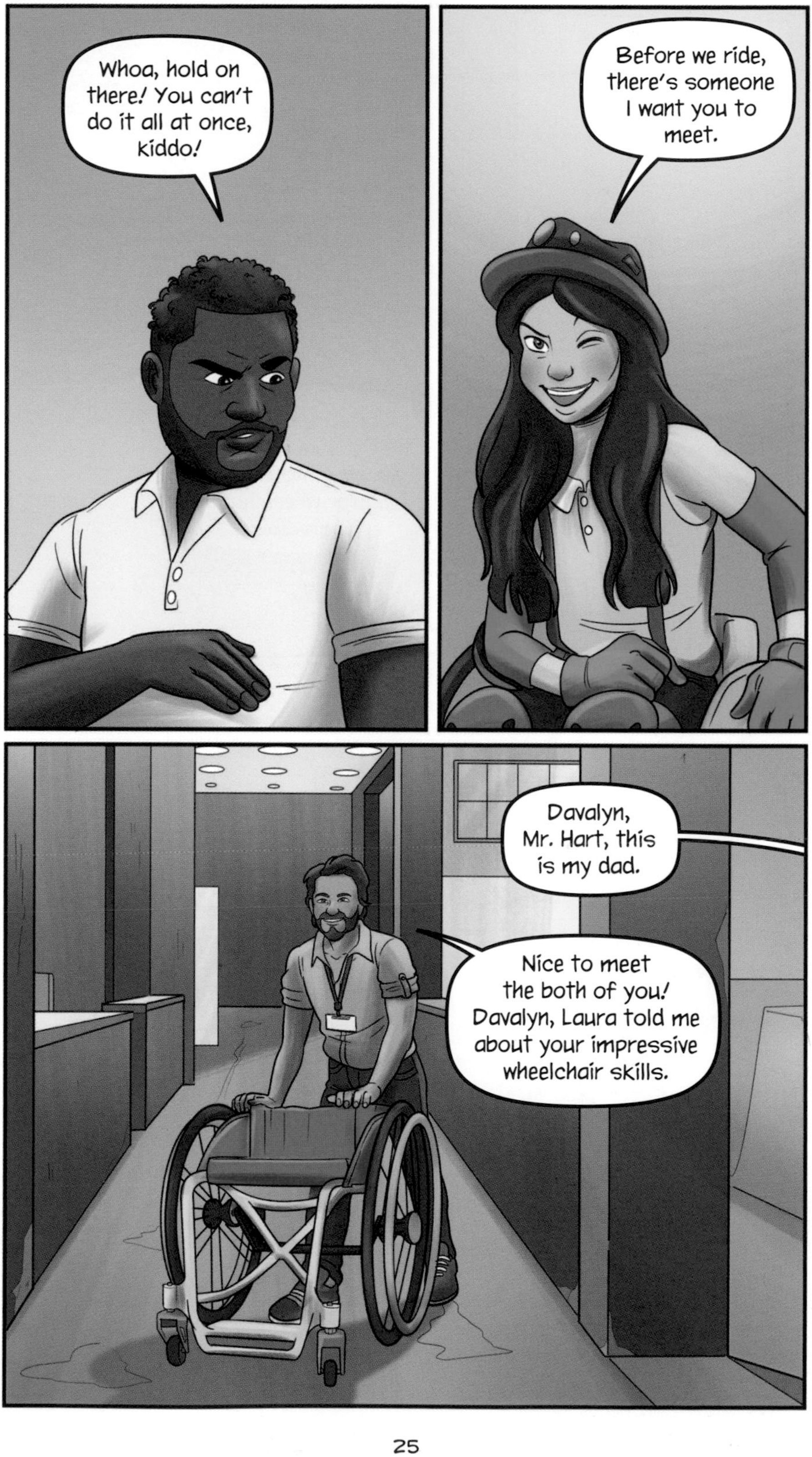

Whoa, hold on there! You can't do it all at once, kiddo!
Before we ride, there's someone I want you to meet.
Davalyn, Mr. Hart, this is my dad.
Nice to meet the both of you! Davalyn, Laura told me about your impressive wheelchair skills.

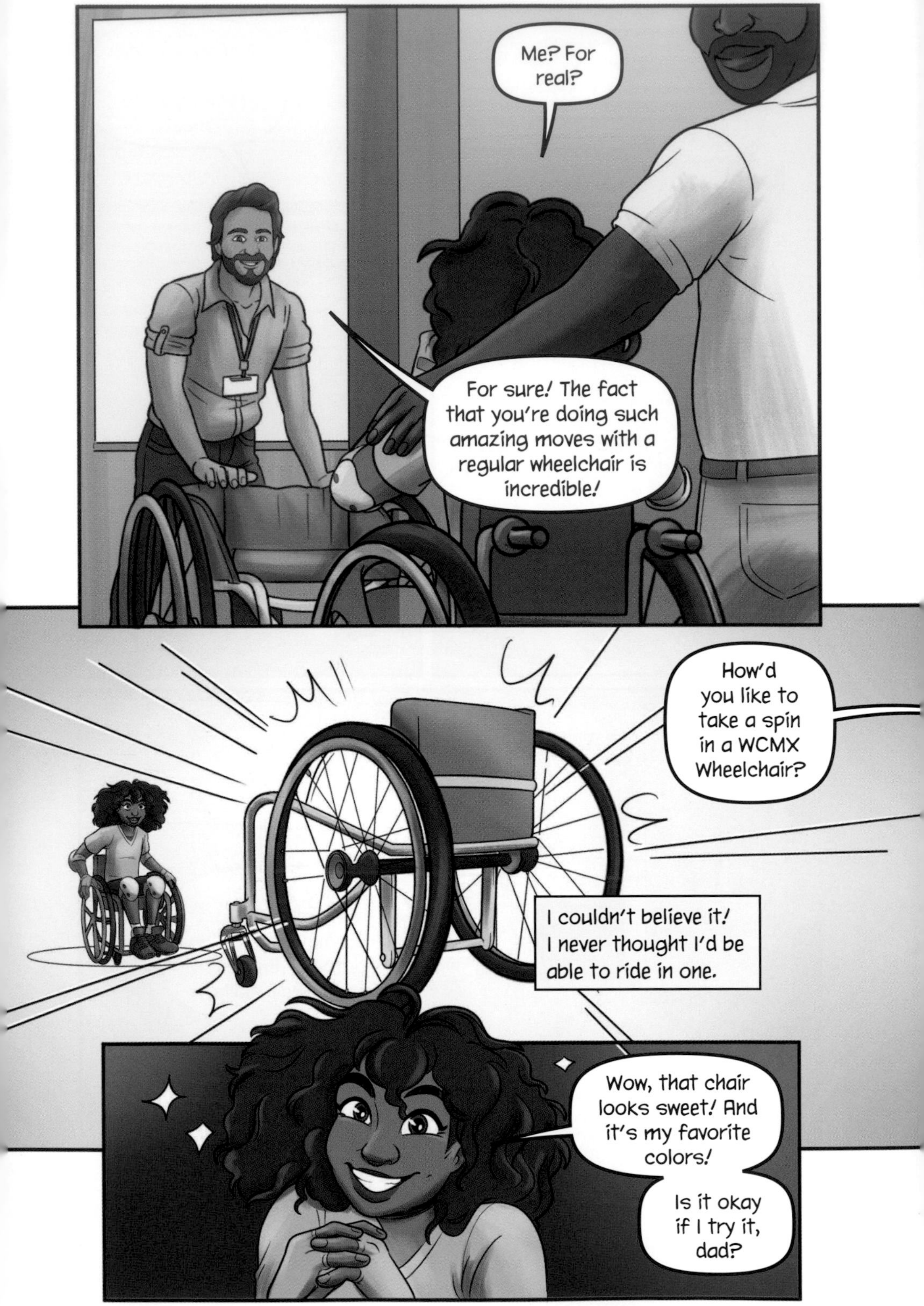
Me? For real?
For sure! The fact that you're doing such amazing moves with a regular wheelchair is incredible!
How'd you like to take a spin in a WCMX Wheelchair?
I couldn't believe it! I never thought I'd be able to ride in one.
Wow, that chair looks sweet! And it's my favorite colors!
Is it okay if I try it, dad?

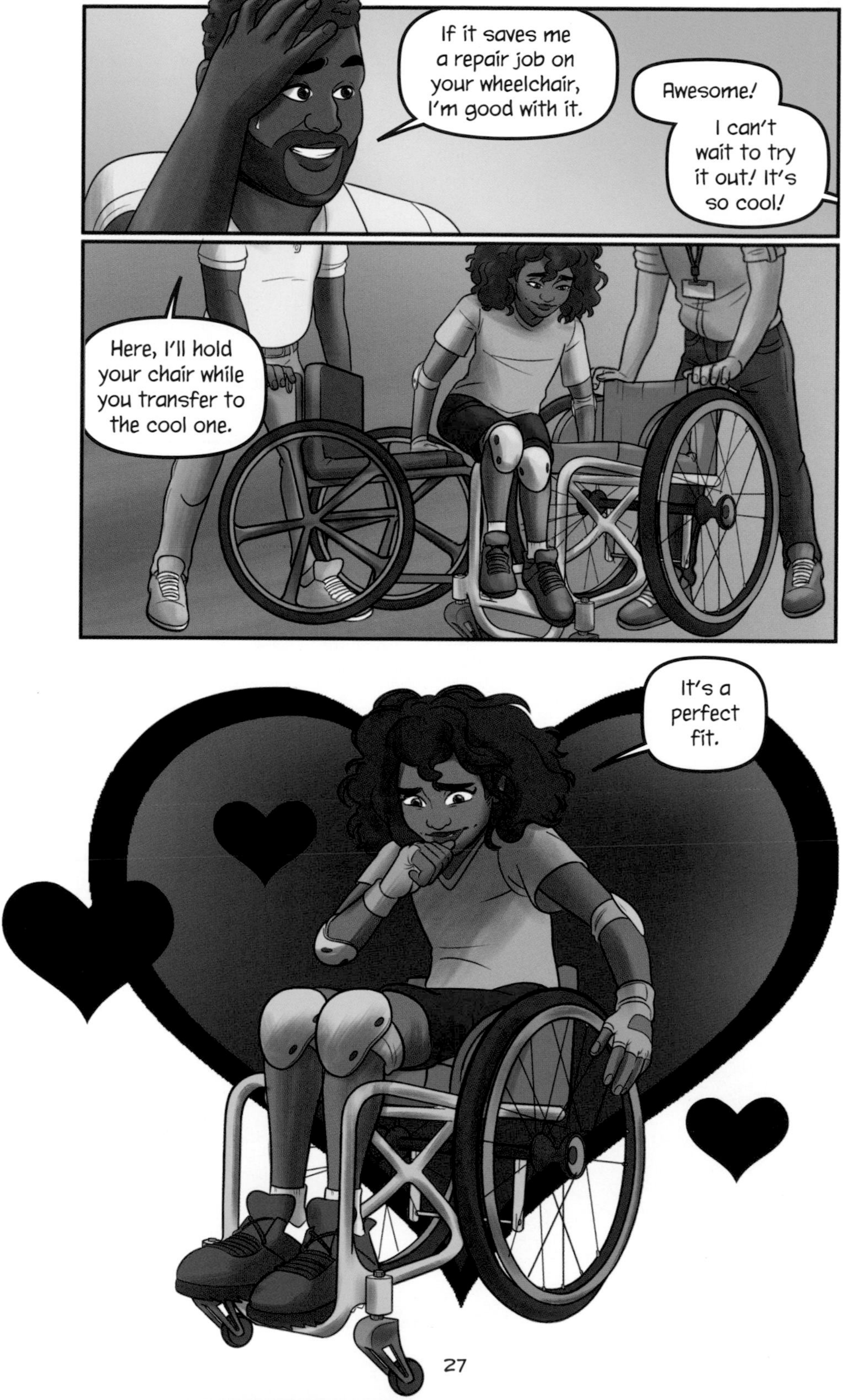
If it saves me a repair job on your wheelchair, I'm good with it.
Awesome!
I can't wait to try it out! It's so cool!
Here, I'll hold your chair while you transfer to the cool one.
It's a perfect fit.

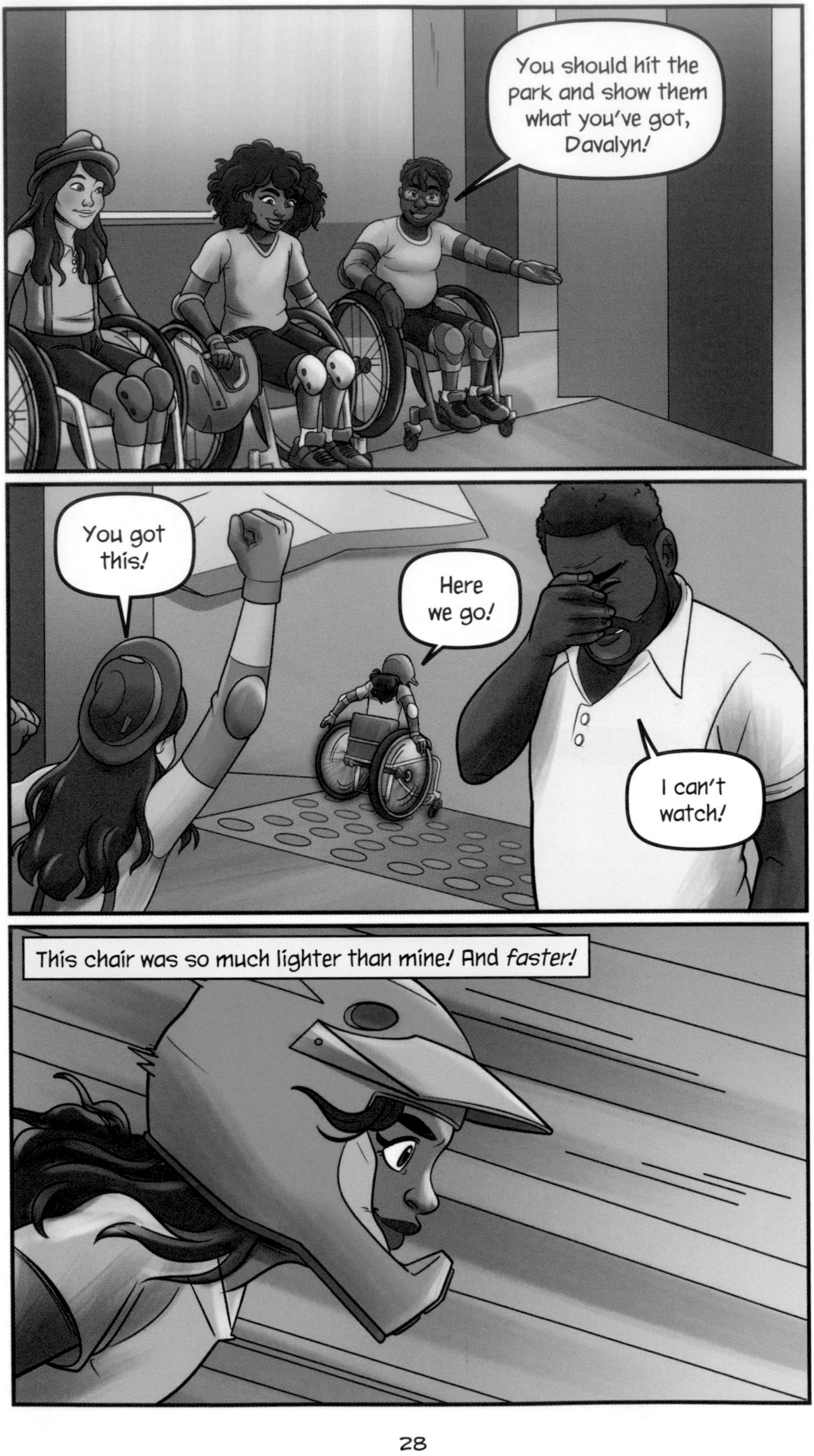
You should hit the park and show them what you've got, Davalyn!
You got this!
Here we go!
I can't watch!
This chair was so much lighter than mine! And *faster!*

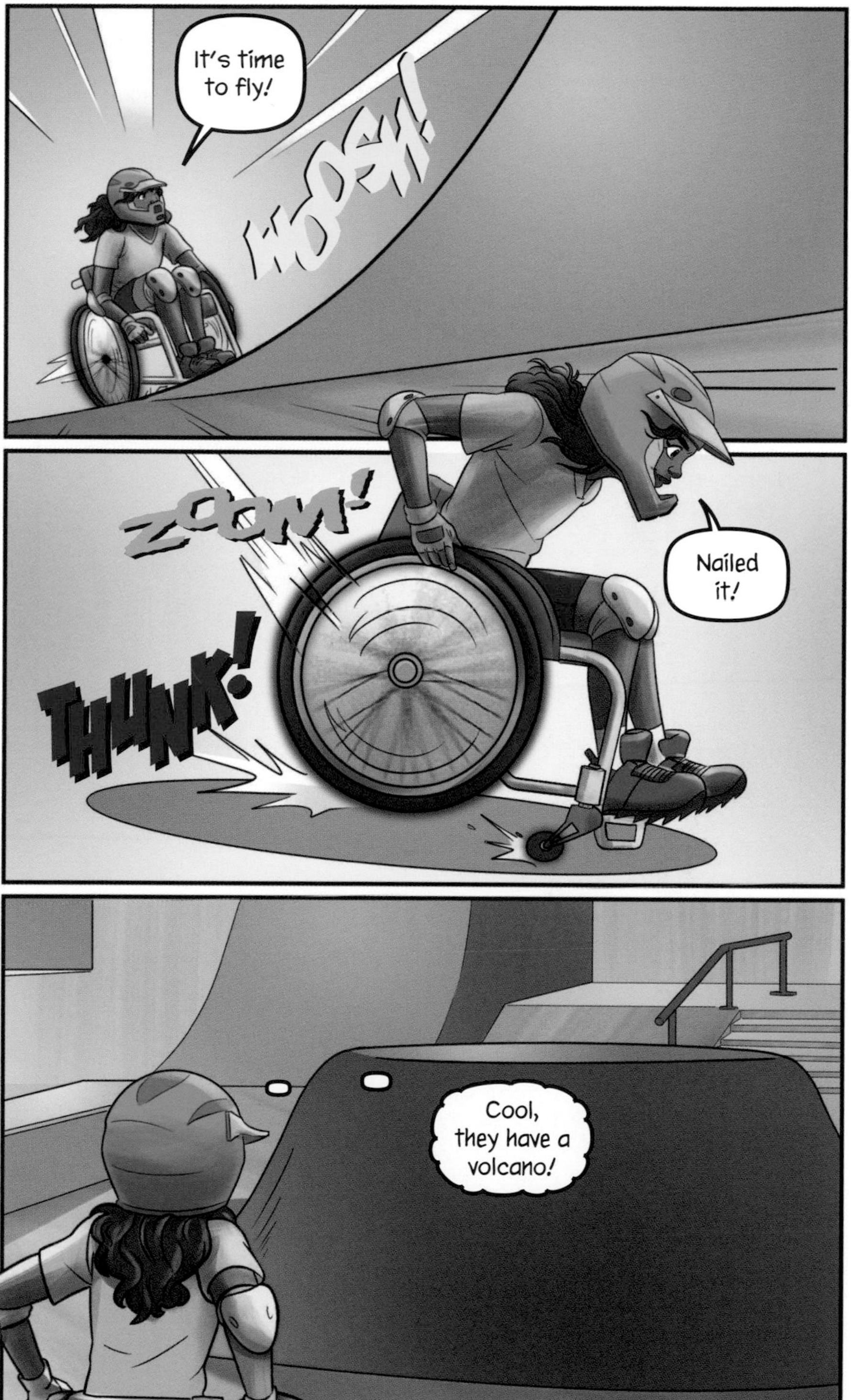
It's time to fly!
WOOSH!
ZOOM!
THUNK!
Nailed it!
Cool, they have a volcano!

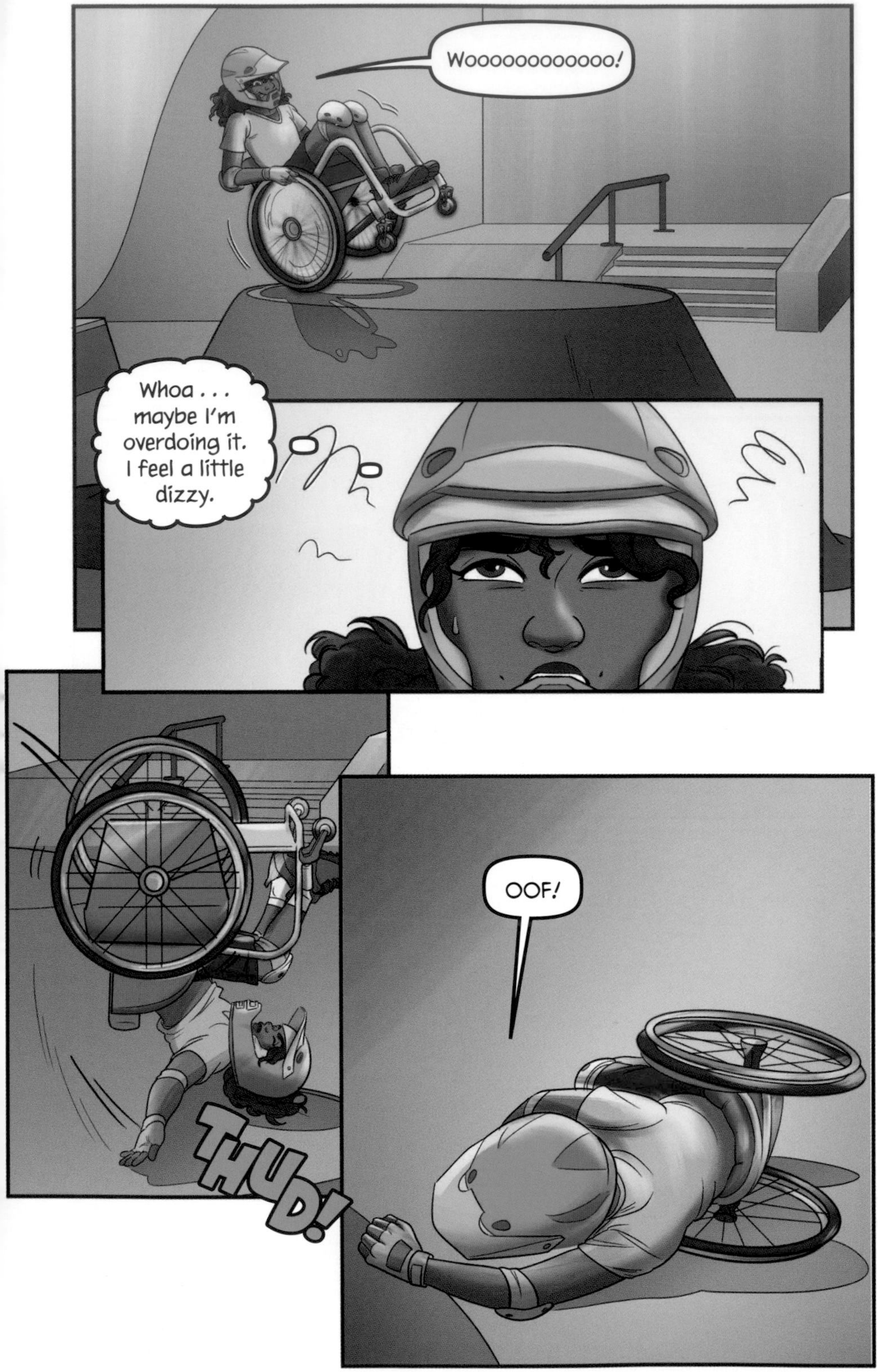
Wooooooooooo!
Whoa . . . maybe I'm overdoing it. I feel a little dizzy.
THUD!
OOF!

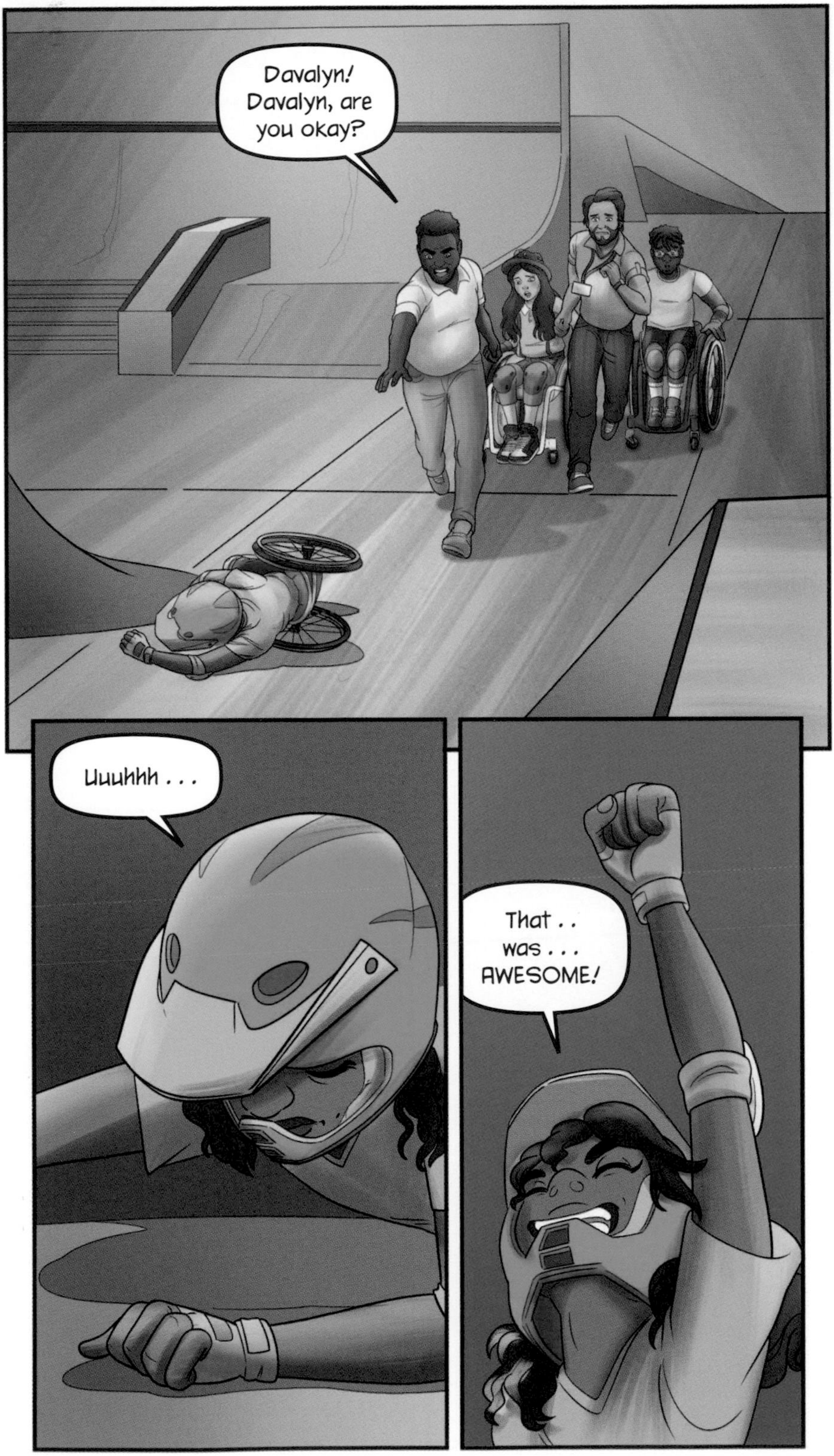
Davalyn! Davalyn, are you okay?
Uuuhhh . . .
That . . was . . . AWESOME!

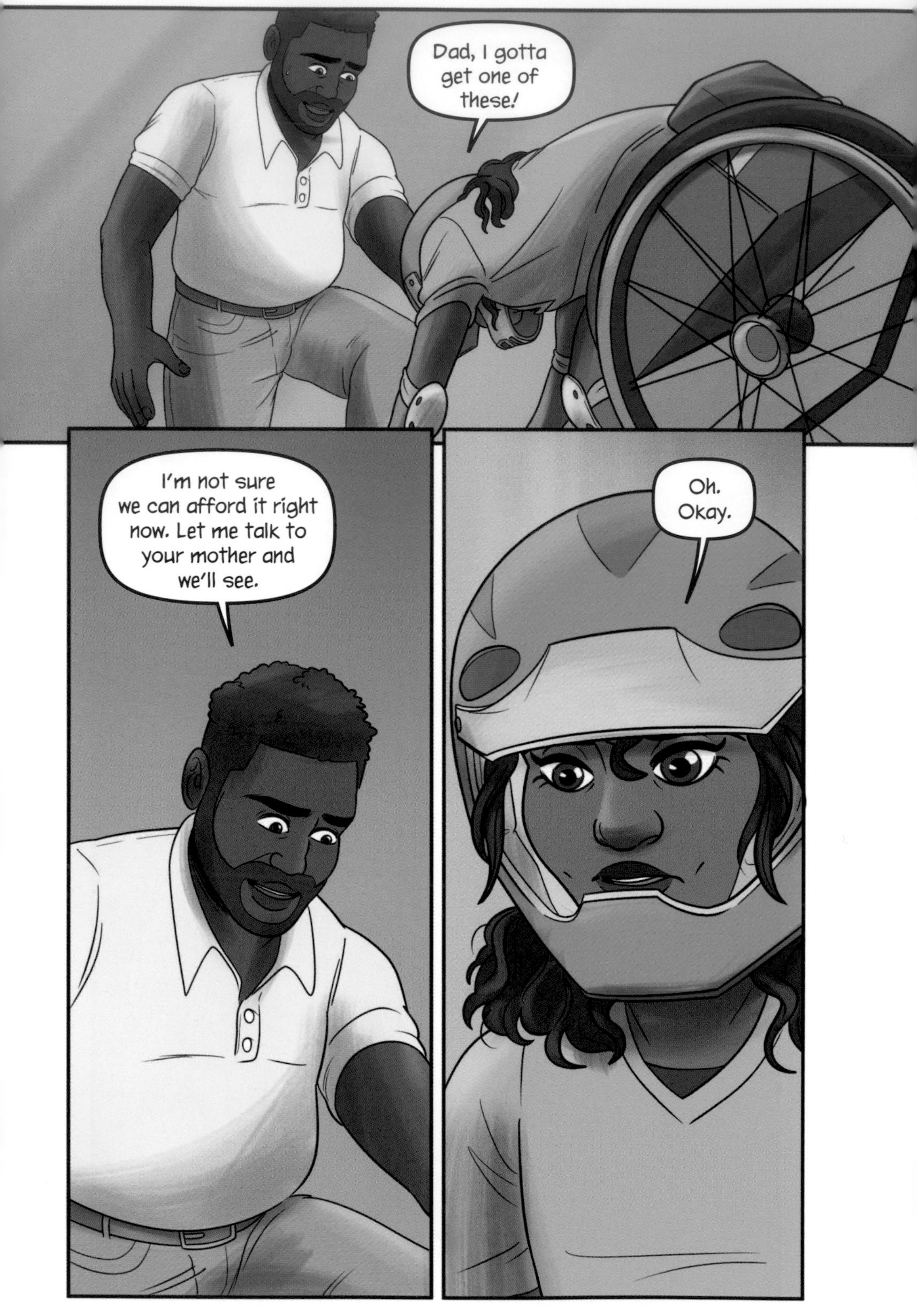
Dad, I gotta get one of these!
I'm not sure we can afford it right now. Let me talk to your mother and we'll see.
Oh. Okay.

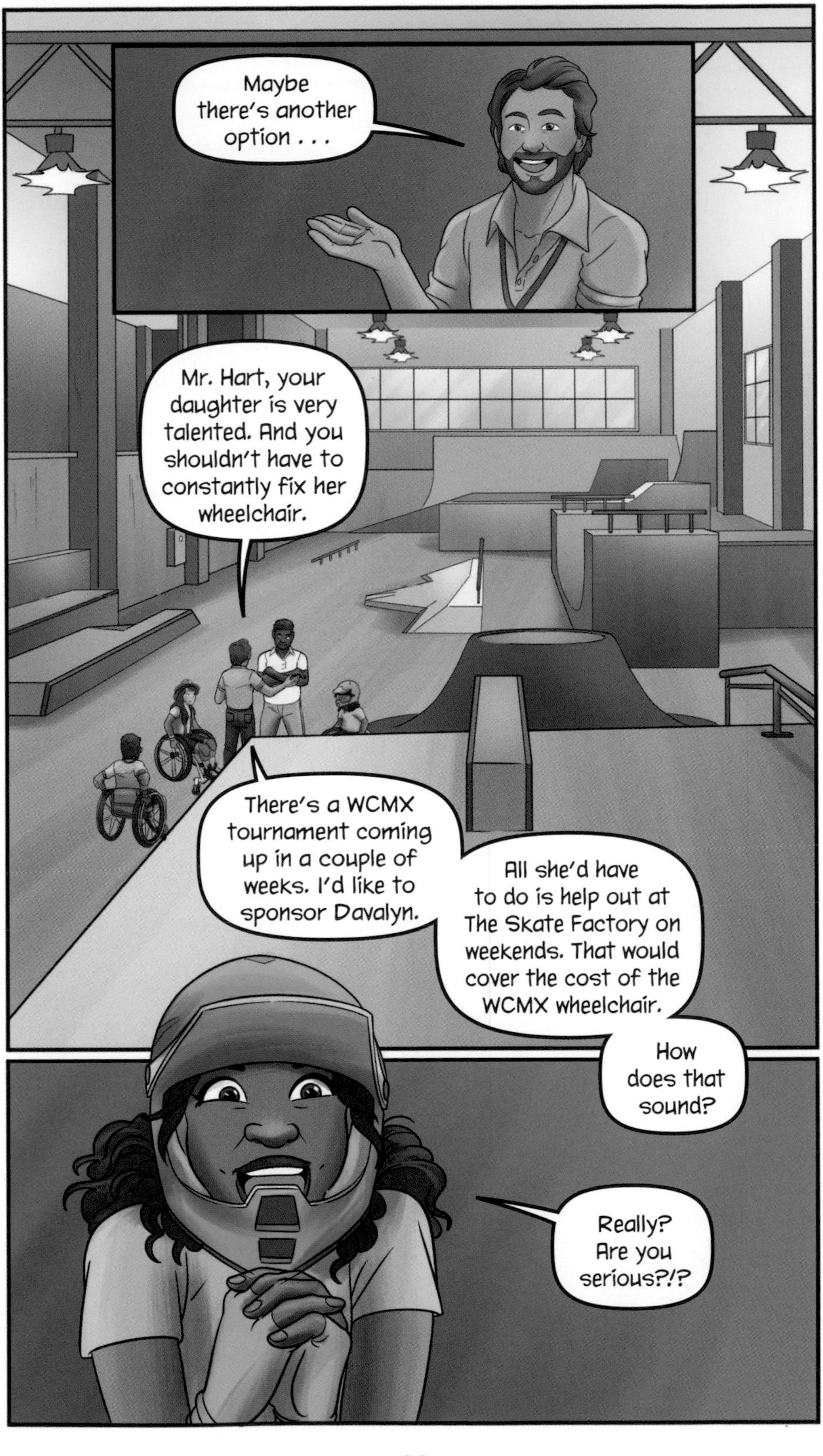
Maybe there's another option . . .
Mr. Hart, your daughter is very talented. And you shouldn't have to constantly fix her wheelchair.
There's a WCMX tournament coming up in a couple of weeks. I'd like to sponsor Davalyn.
All she'd have to do is help out at The Skate Factory on weekends. That would cover the cost of the WCMX wheelchair.
How does that sound?
Really? Are you serious?!?

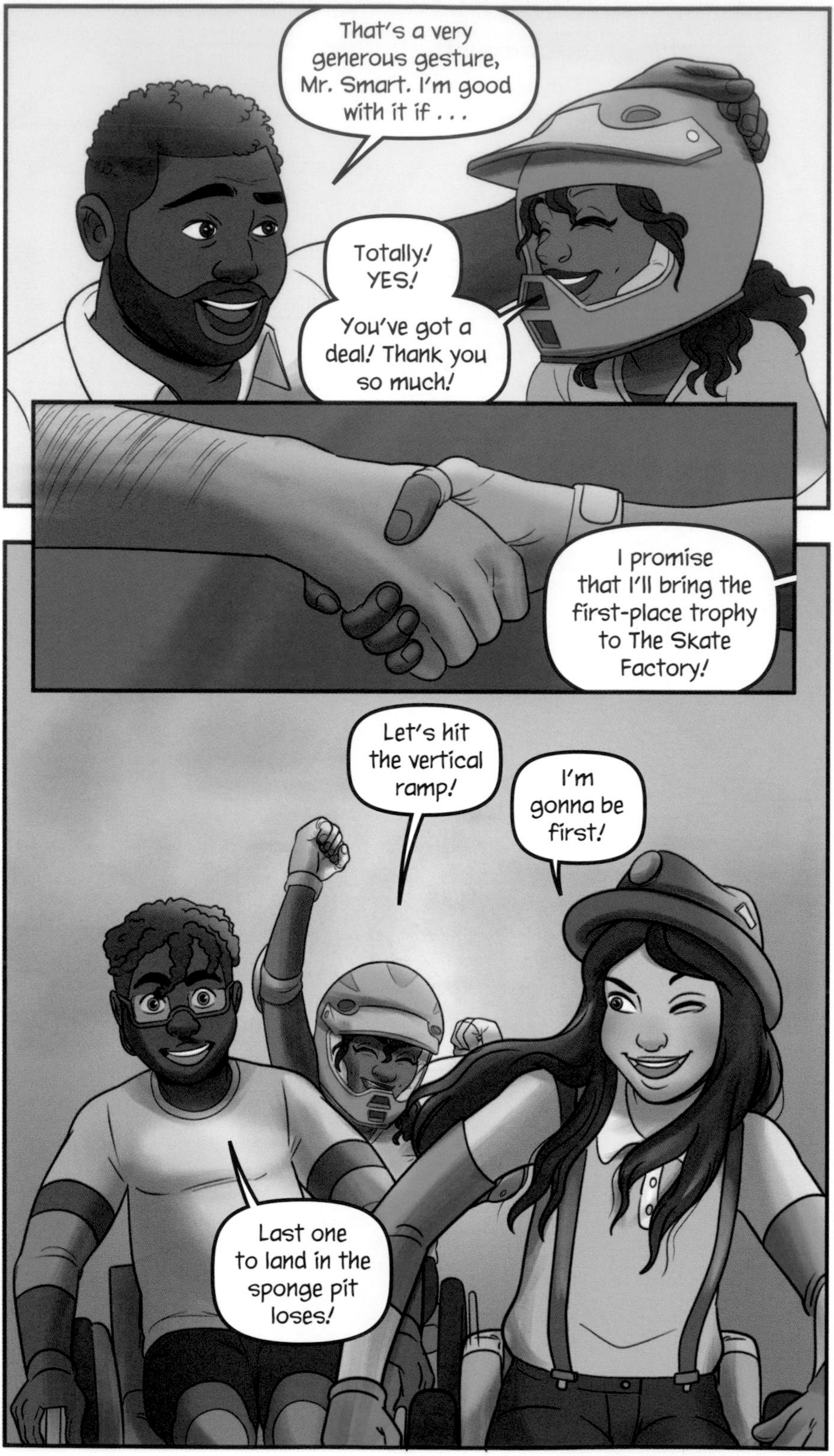
That's a very generous gesture, Mr. Smart. I'm good with it if . . .
Totally! YES!
You've got a deal! Thank you so much!
I promise that I'll bring the first-place trophy to The Skate Factory!
Let's hit the vertical ramp!
I'm gonna be first!
Last one to land in the sponge pit loses!

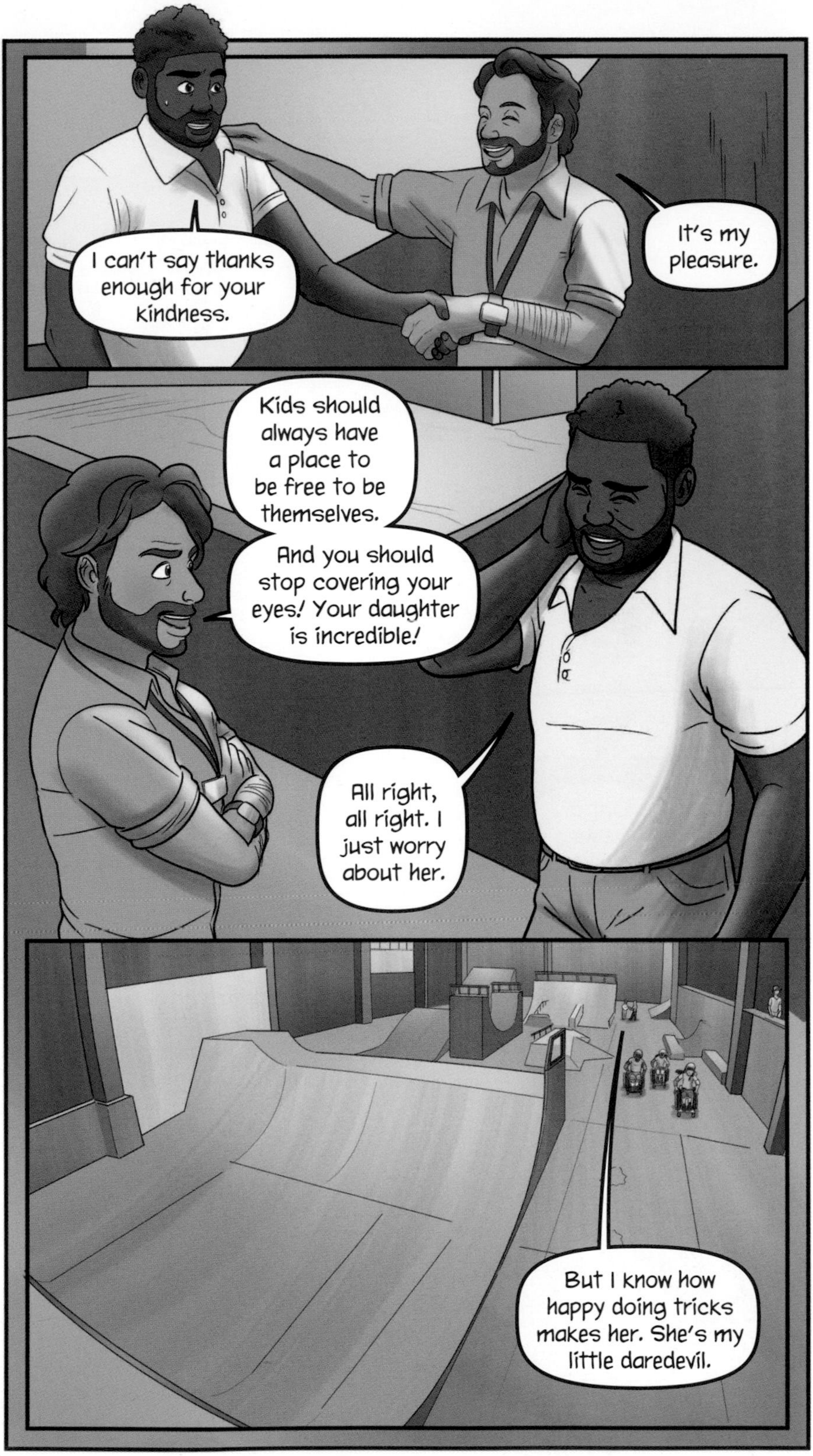
I can't say thanks enough for your kindness.
It's my pleasure.
Kids should always have a place to be free to be themselves.
And you should stop covering your eyes! Your daughter is incredible!
All right, all right. I just worry about her.
But I know how happy doing tricks makes her. She's my little daredevil.

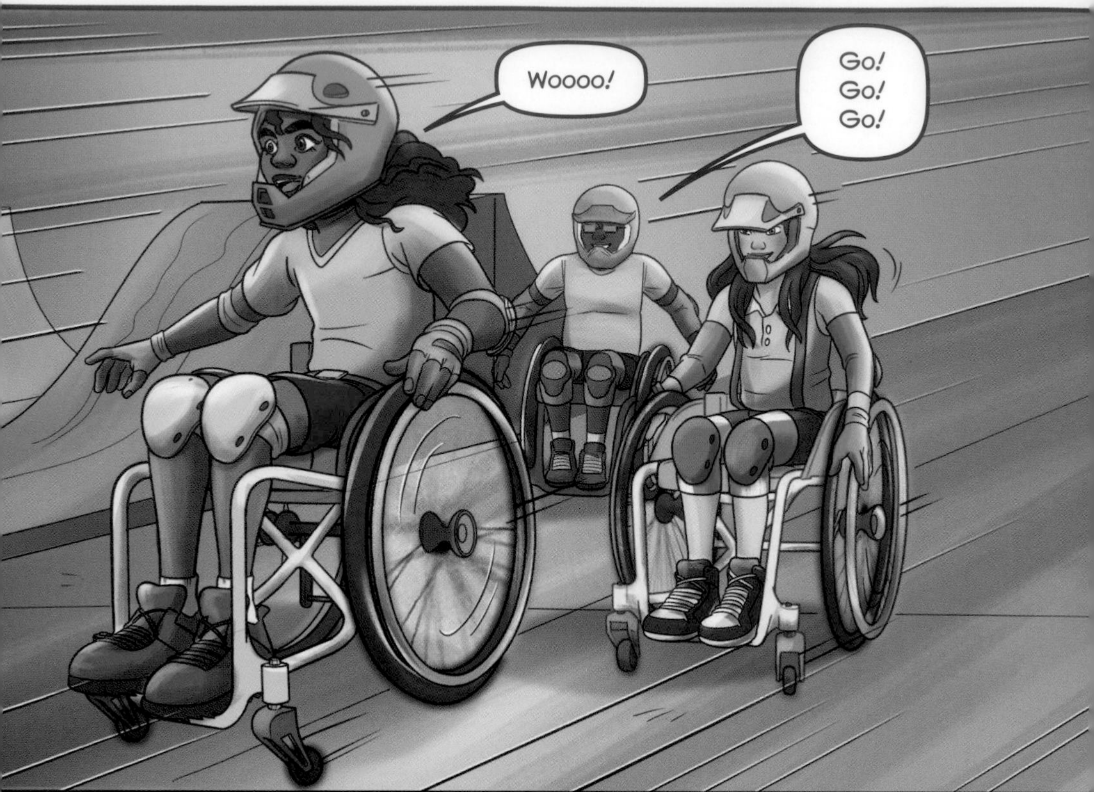
Woooo!
Go! Go! Go!

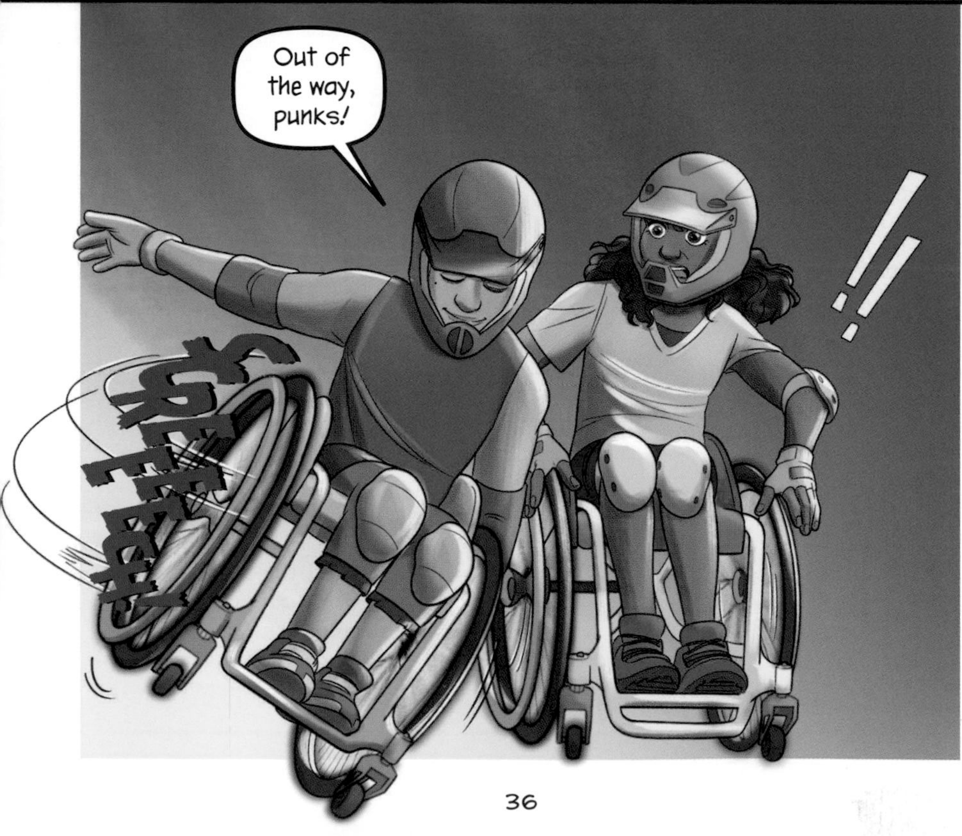
Out of the way, punks!
SCREEEECH!
!!

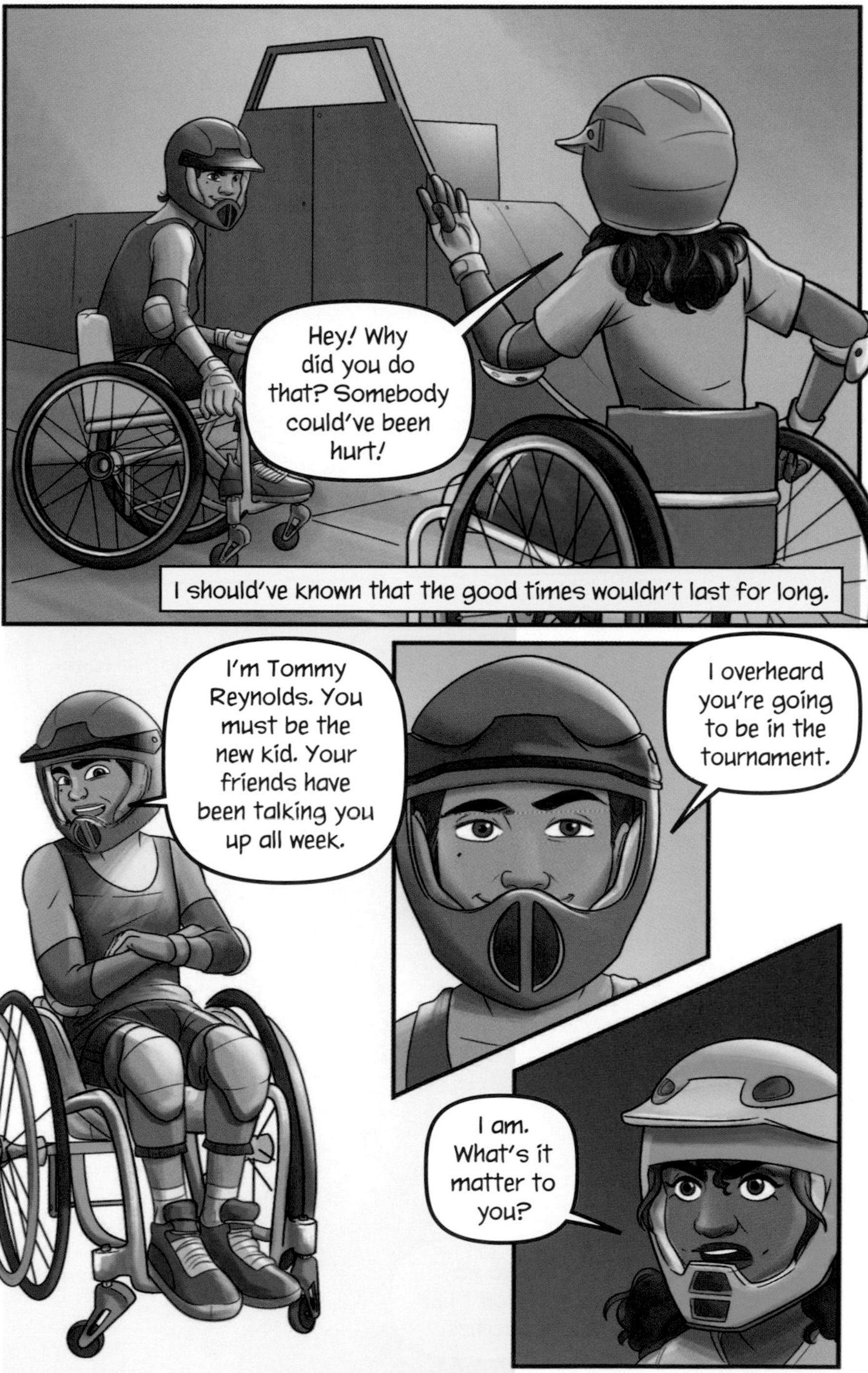
Hey! Why did you do that? Somebody could've been hurt!
I should've known that the good times wouldn't last for long.
I'm Tommy Reynolds. You must be the new kid. Your friends have been talking you up all week.
I overheard you're going to be in the tournament.
I am. What's it matter to you?

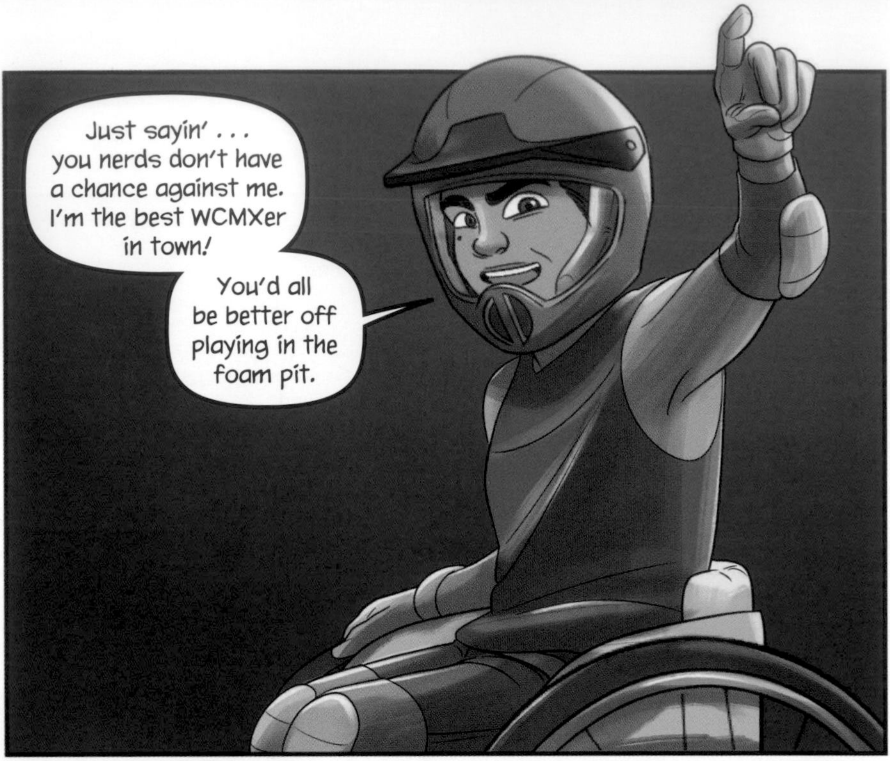
Just sayin' . . . you nerds don't have a chance against me. I'm the best WCMXer in town!
You'd all be better off playing in the foam pit.

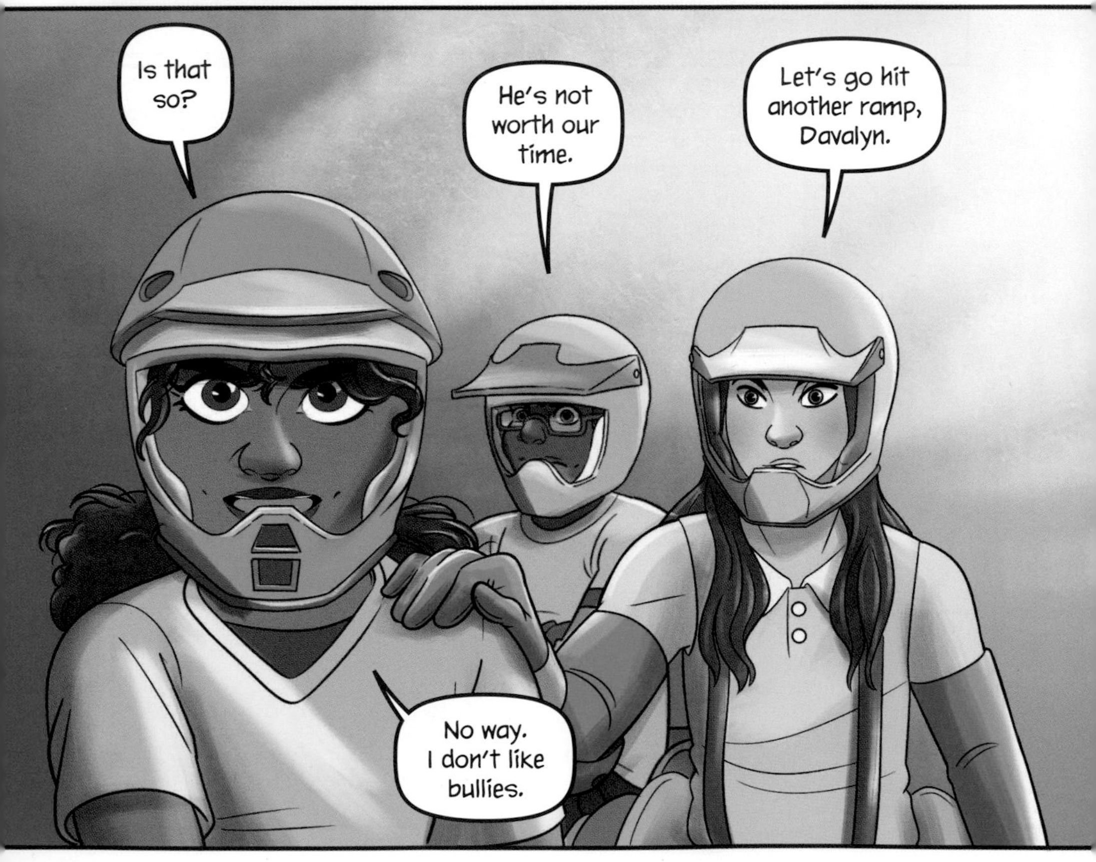
Is that so?
He's not worth our time.
Let's go hit another ramp, Davalyn.
No way. I don't like bullies.

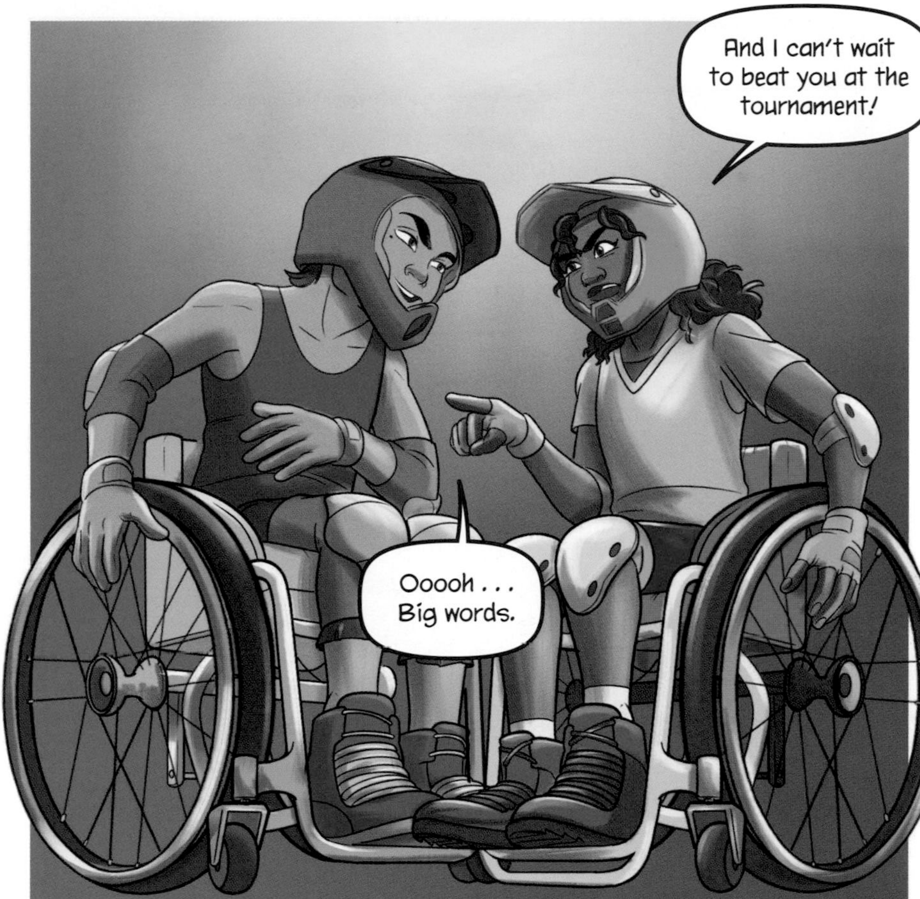
And I can't wait to beat you at the tournament!
Ooooh . . . Big words.

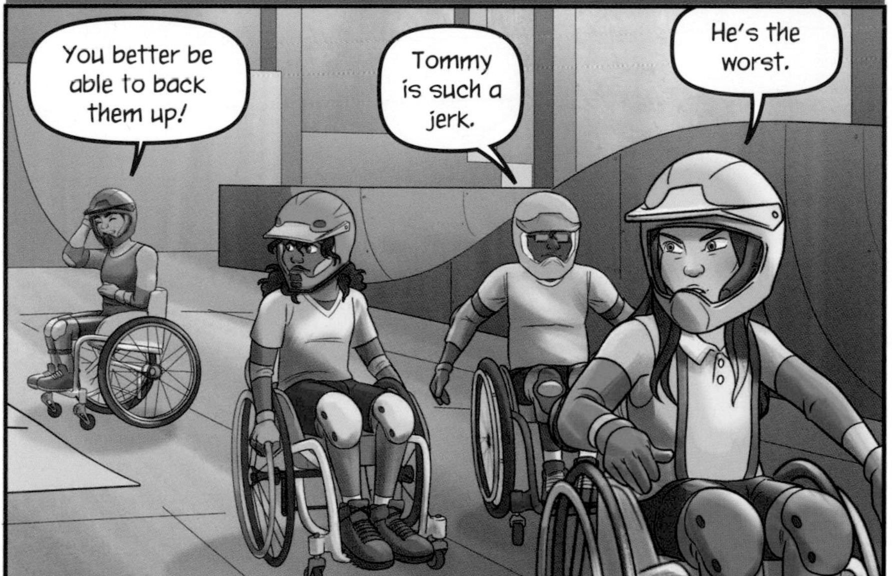
You better be able to back them up!
Tommy is such a jerk.
He's the worst.

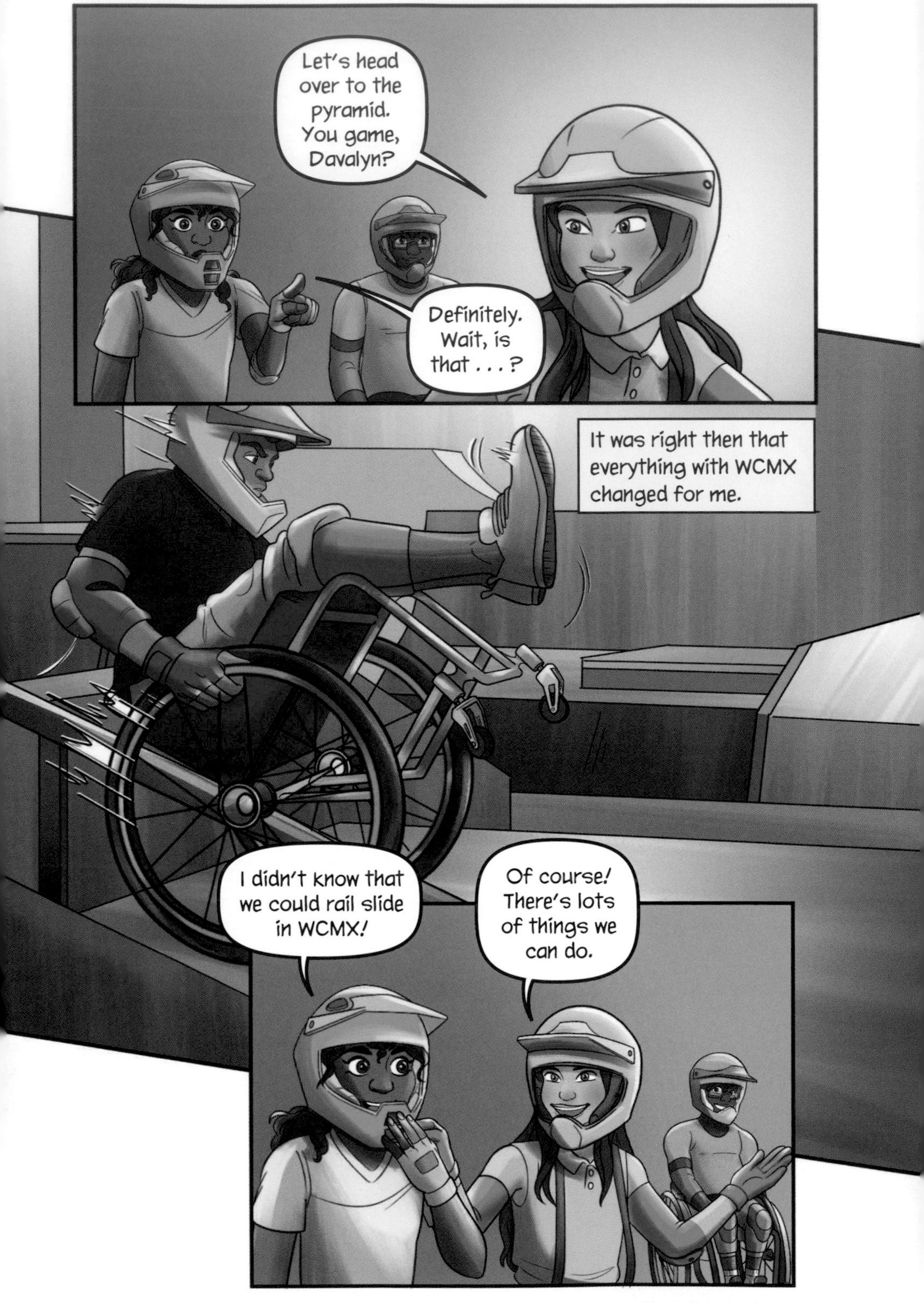
Let's head over to the pyramid. You game, Davalyn?
Definitely. Wait, is that . . . ?
It was right then that everything with WCMX changed for me.
I didn't know that we could rail slide in WCMX!
Of course! There's lots of things we can do.

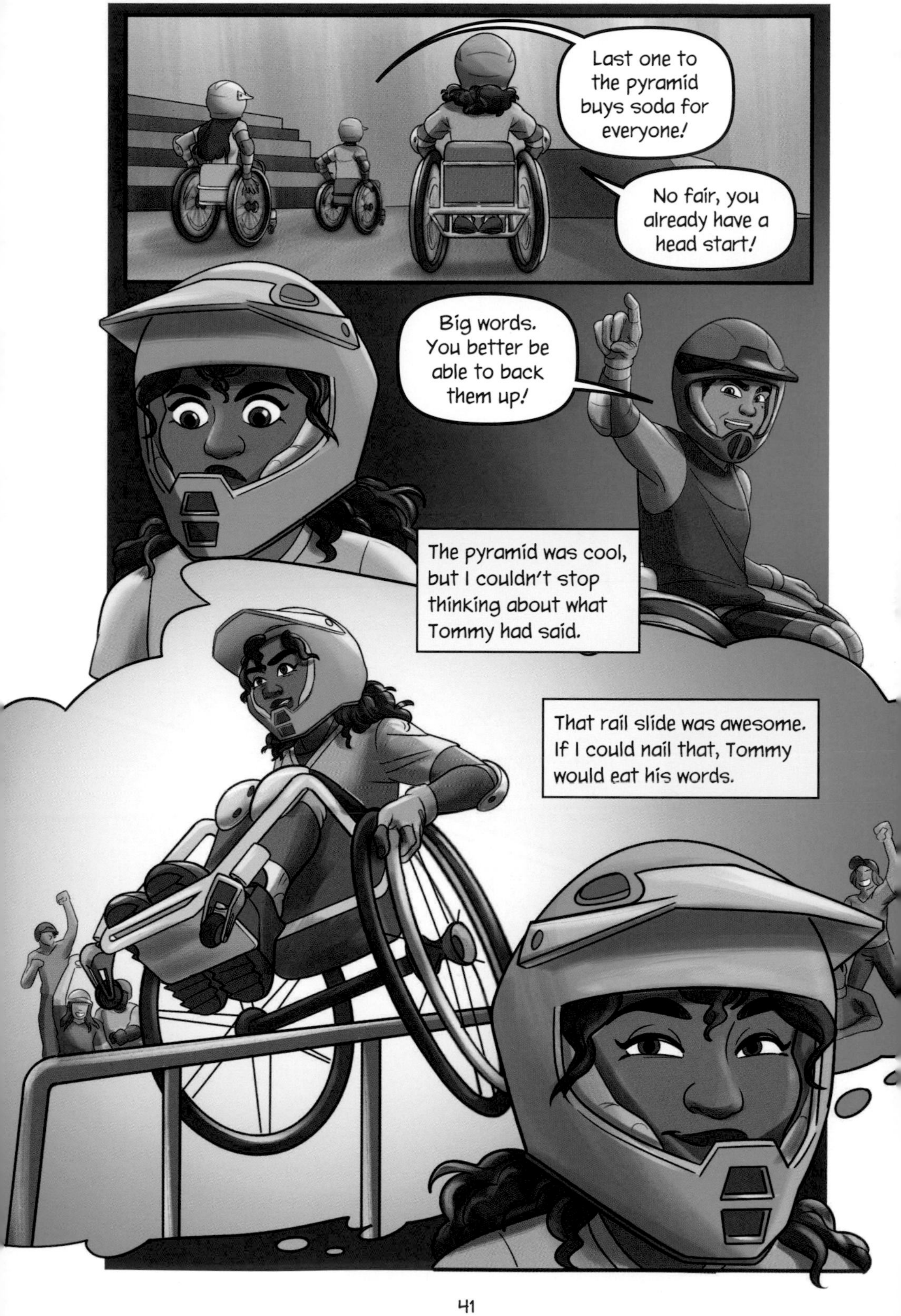
Last one to the pyramid buys soda for everyone!
No fair, you already have a head start!
Big words. You better be able to back them up!
The pyramid was cool, but I couldn't stop thinking about what Tommy had said.
That rail slide was awesome. If I could nail that, Tommy would eat his words.

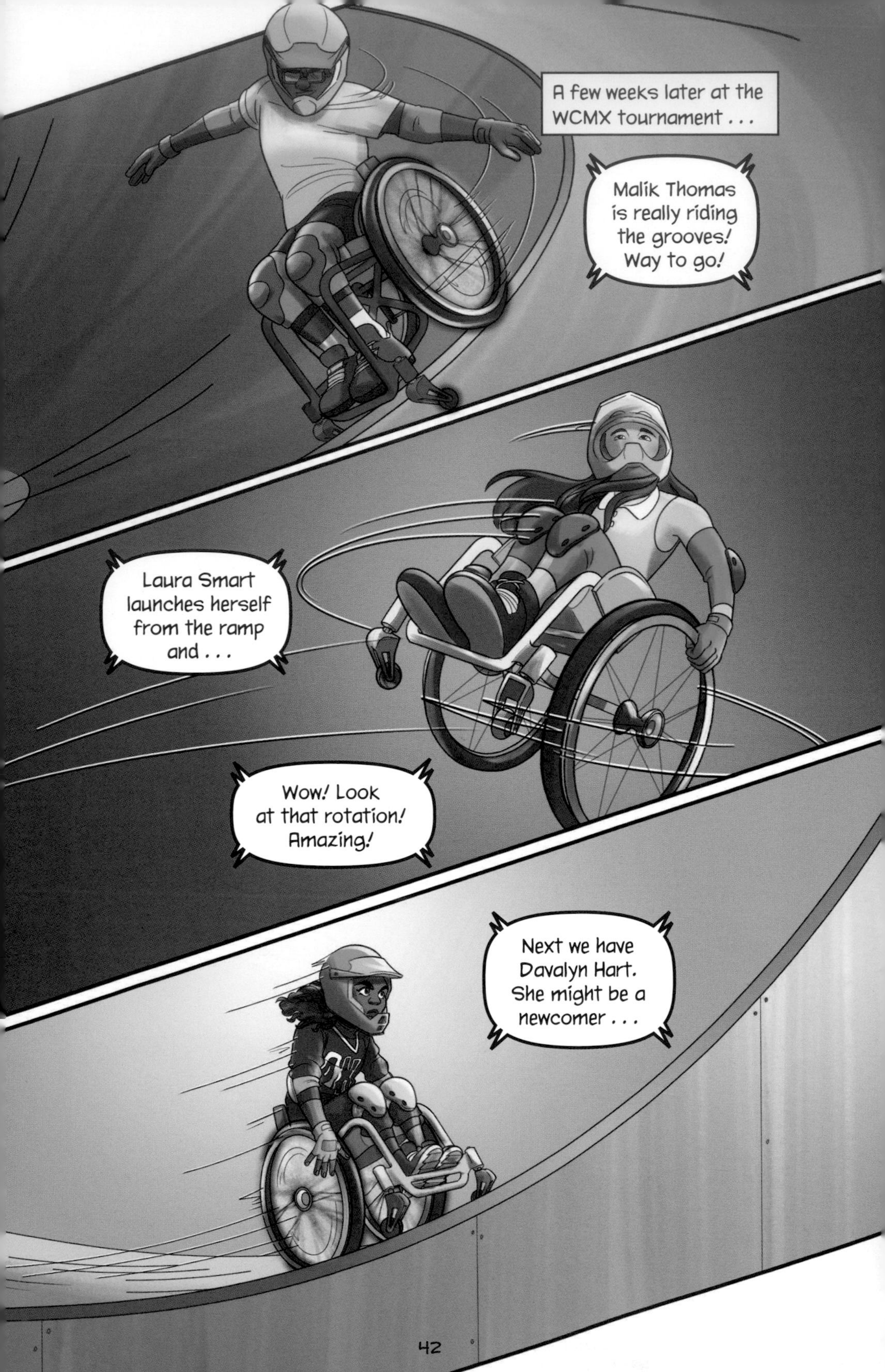
A few weeks later at the WCMX tournament . . .
Malik Thomas is really riding the grooves! Way to go!
Laura Smart launches herself from the ramp and . . .
Wow! Look at that rotation! Amazing!
Next we have Davalyn Hart. She might be a newcomer . . .

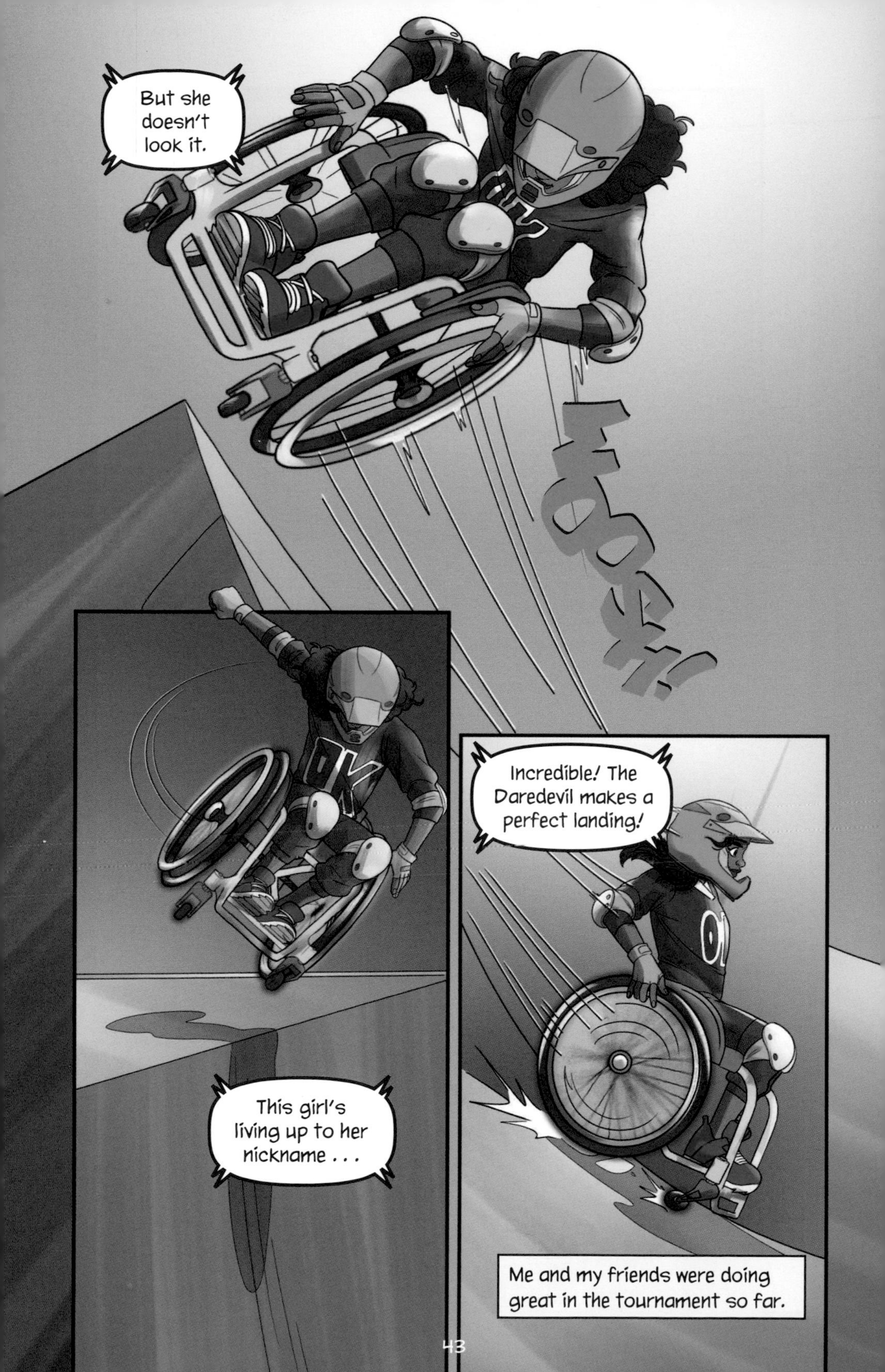
But she doesn't look it.
WHOOSH!
This girl's living up to her nickname . . .
Incredible! The Daredevil makes a perfect landing!
Me and my friends were doing great in the tournament so far.

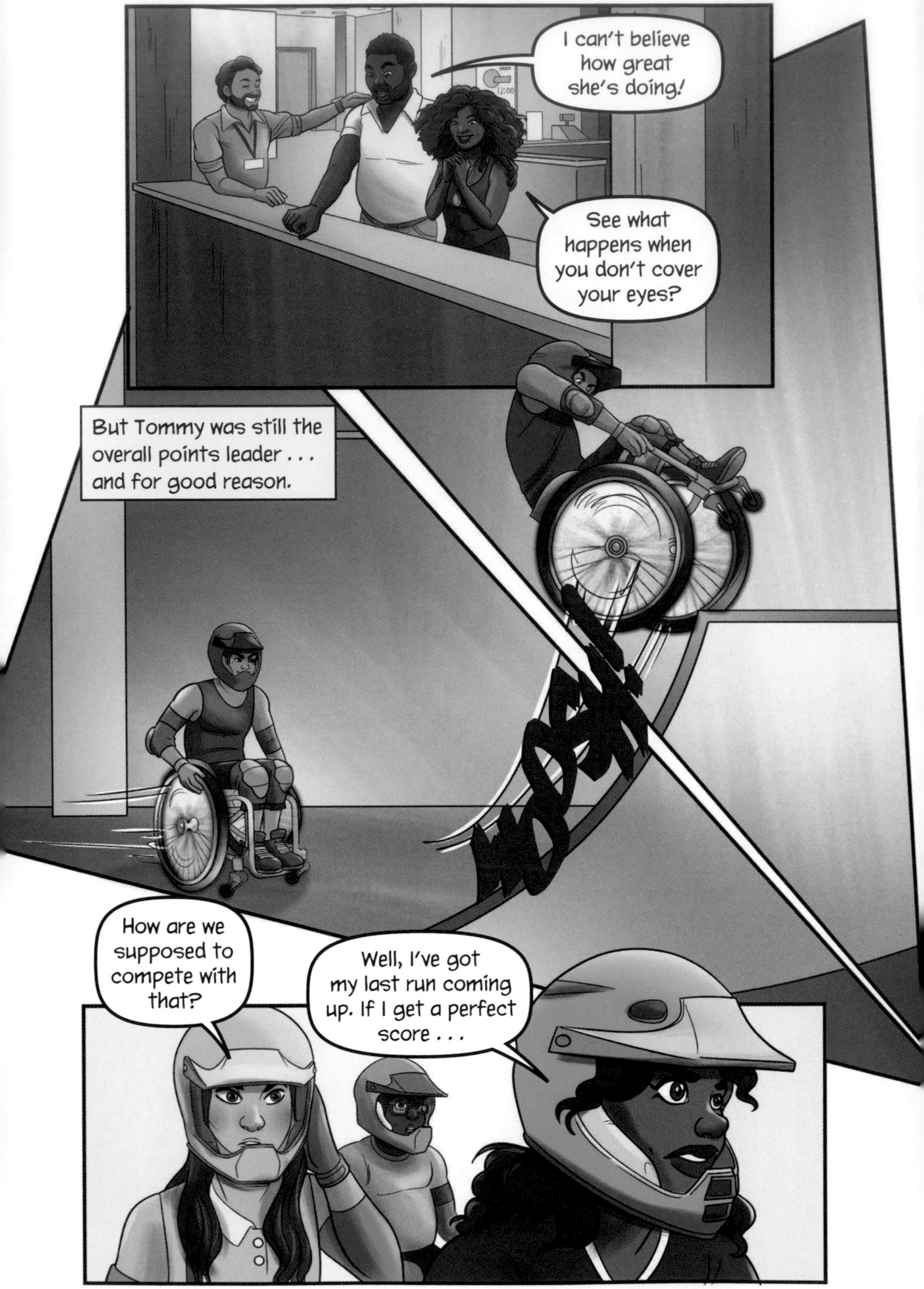
I can't believe how great she's doing!
See what happens when you don't cover your eyes?
But Tommy was still the overall points leader . . . and for good reason.
WOOSH!
How are we supposed to compete with that?
Well, I've got my last run coming up. If I get a perfect score . . .

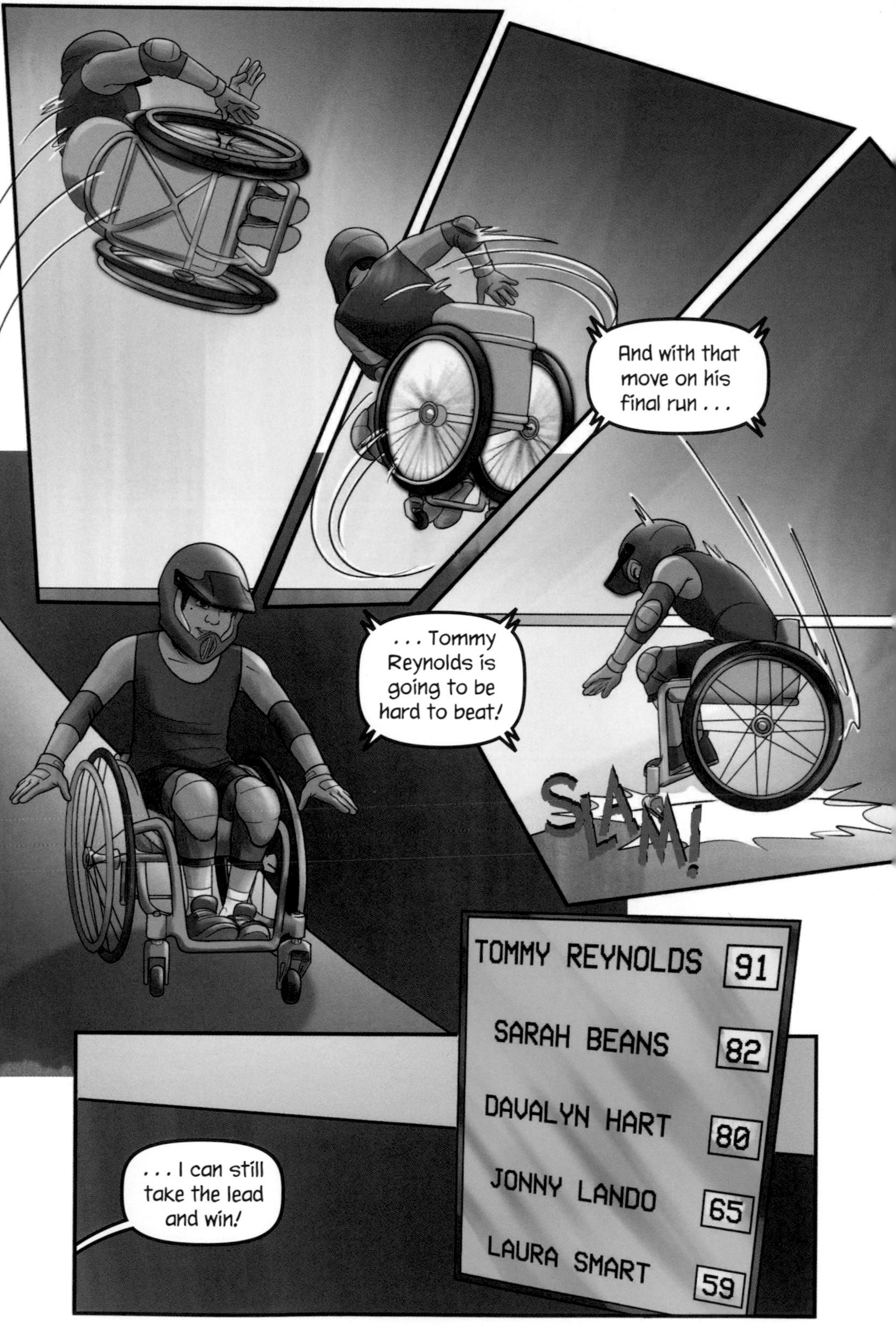
And with that move on his final run . . .
. . . Tommy Reynolds is going to be hard to beat!
SLAM!
TOMMY REYNOLDS 91
SARAH BEANS 82
DAVALYN HART 80
JONNY LANDO 65
LAURA SMART 59
. . . I can still take the lead and win!

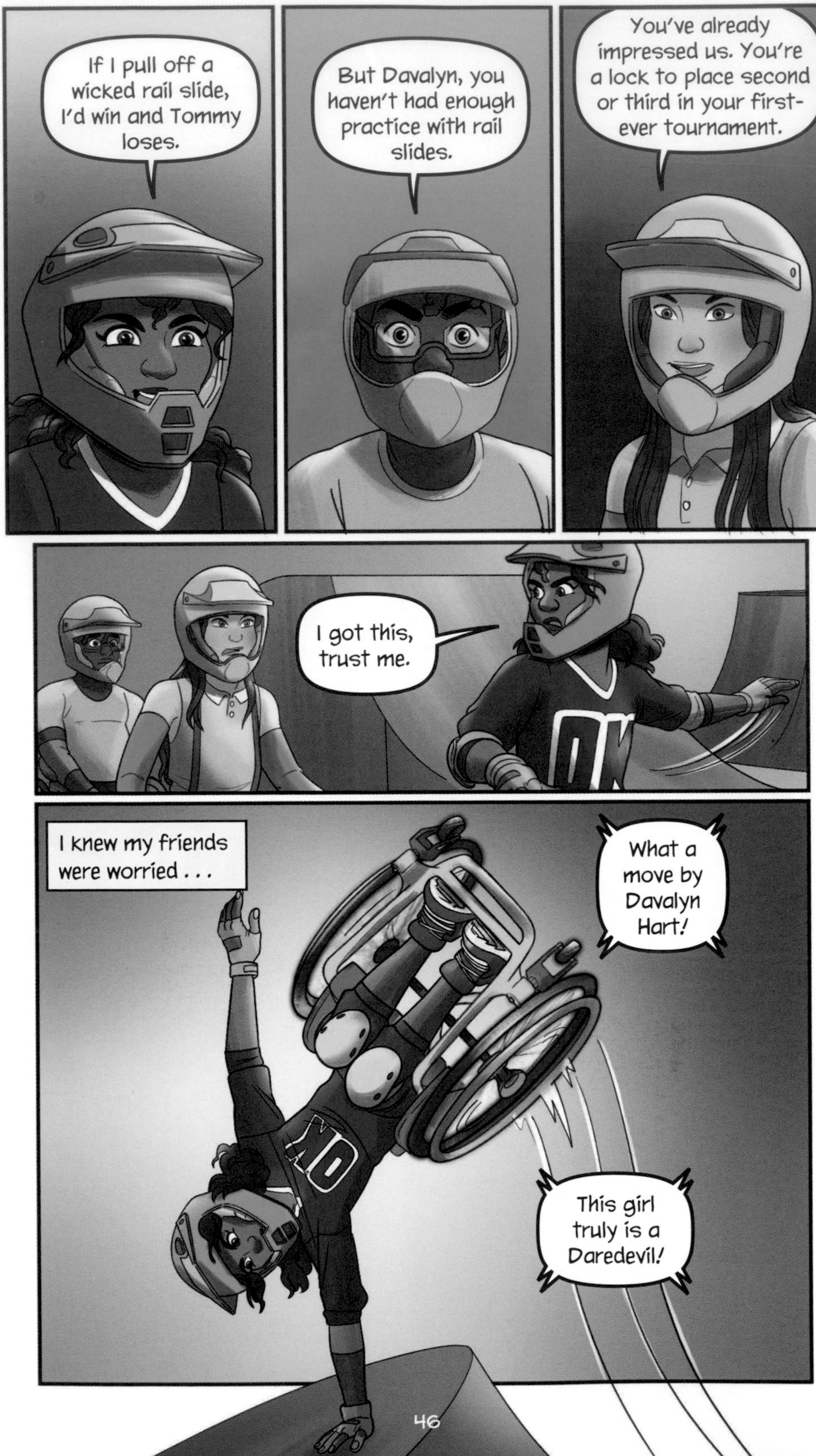
If I pull off a wicked rail slide, I'd win and Tommy loses.
But Davalyn, you haven't had enough practice with rail slides.
You've already impressed us. You're a lock to place second or third in your first-ever tournament.
I got this, trust me.
I knew my friends were worried . . .
What a move by Davalyn Hart!
This girl truly is a Daredevil!

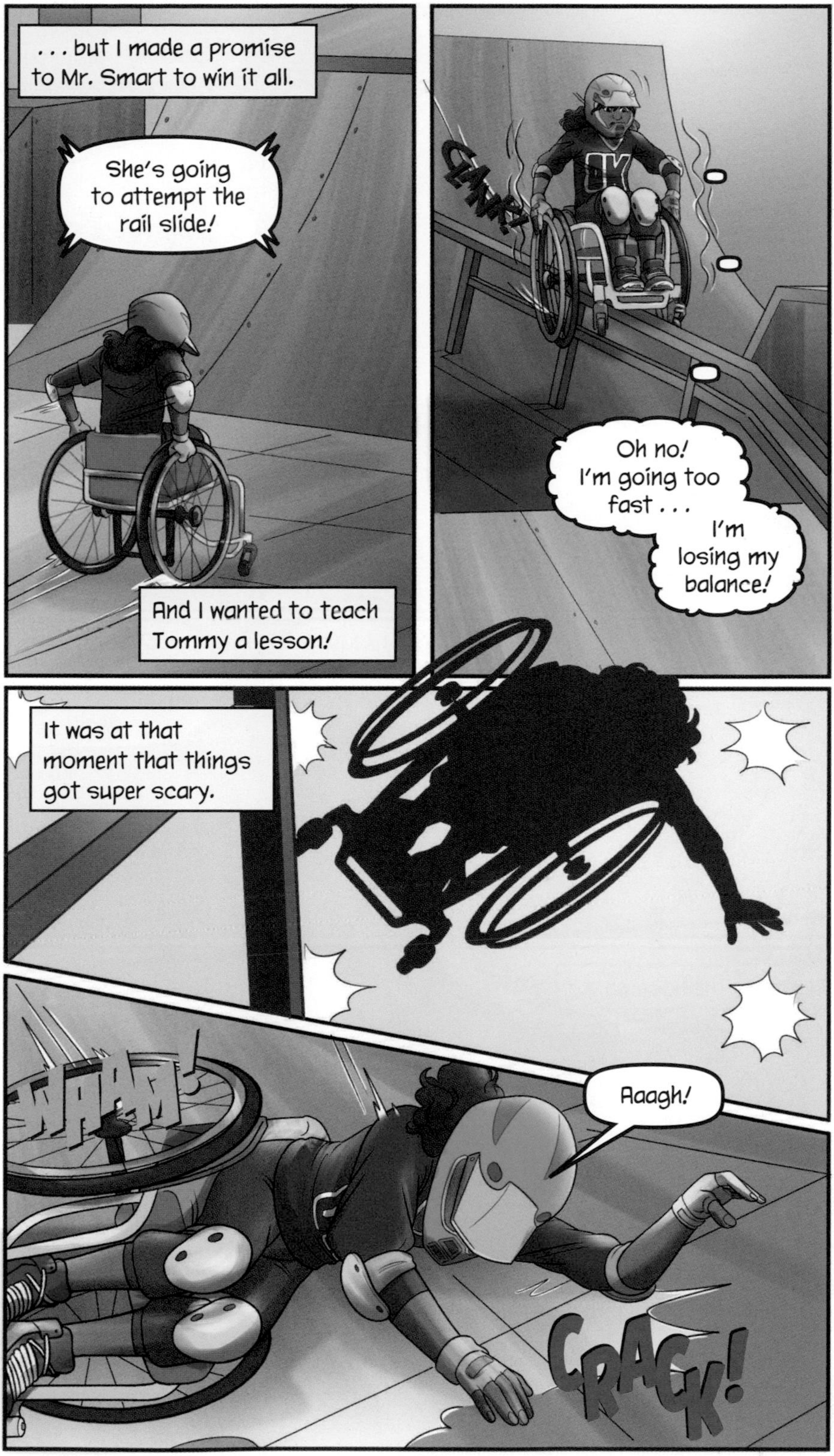
. . . but I made a promise to Mr. Smart to win it all.
She's going to attempt the rail slide!
And I wanted to teach Tommy a lesson!
CLANK!
Oh no! I'm going too fast . . .
I'm losing my balance!
It was at that moment that things got super scary.
WHAM!
Aaagh!
CRACK!

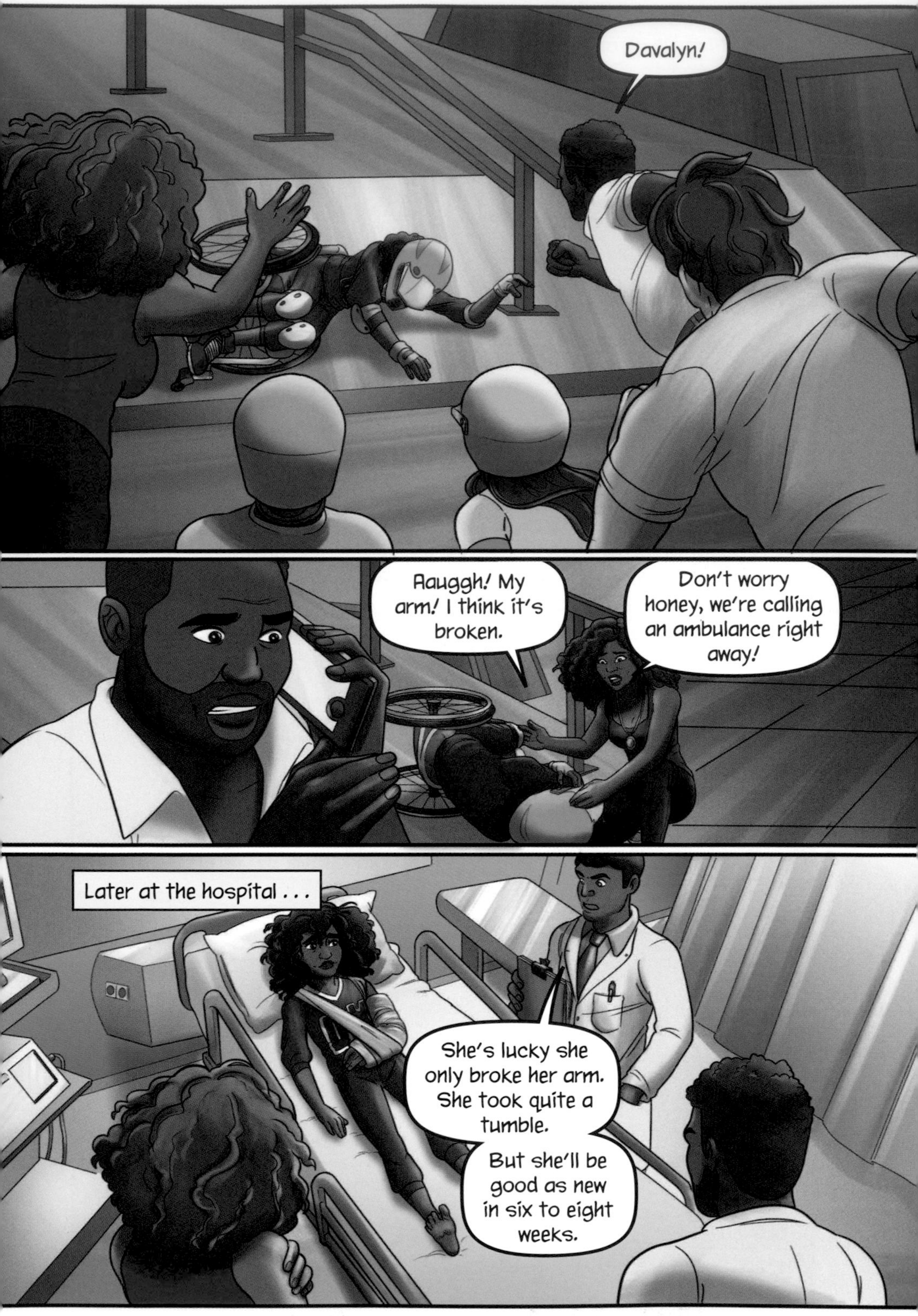
Davalyn!
Aauggh! My arm! I think it's broken.
Don't worry honey, we're calling an ambulance right away!
Later at the hospital . . .
She's lucky she only broke her arm. She took quite a tumble.
But she'll be good as new in six to eight weeks.

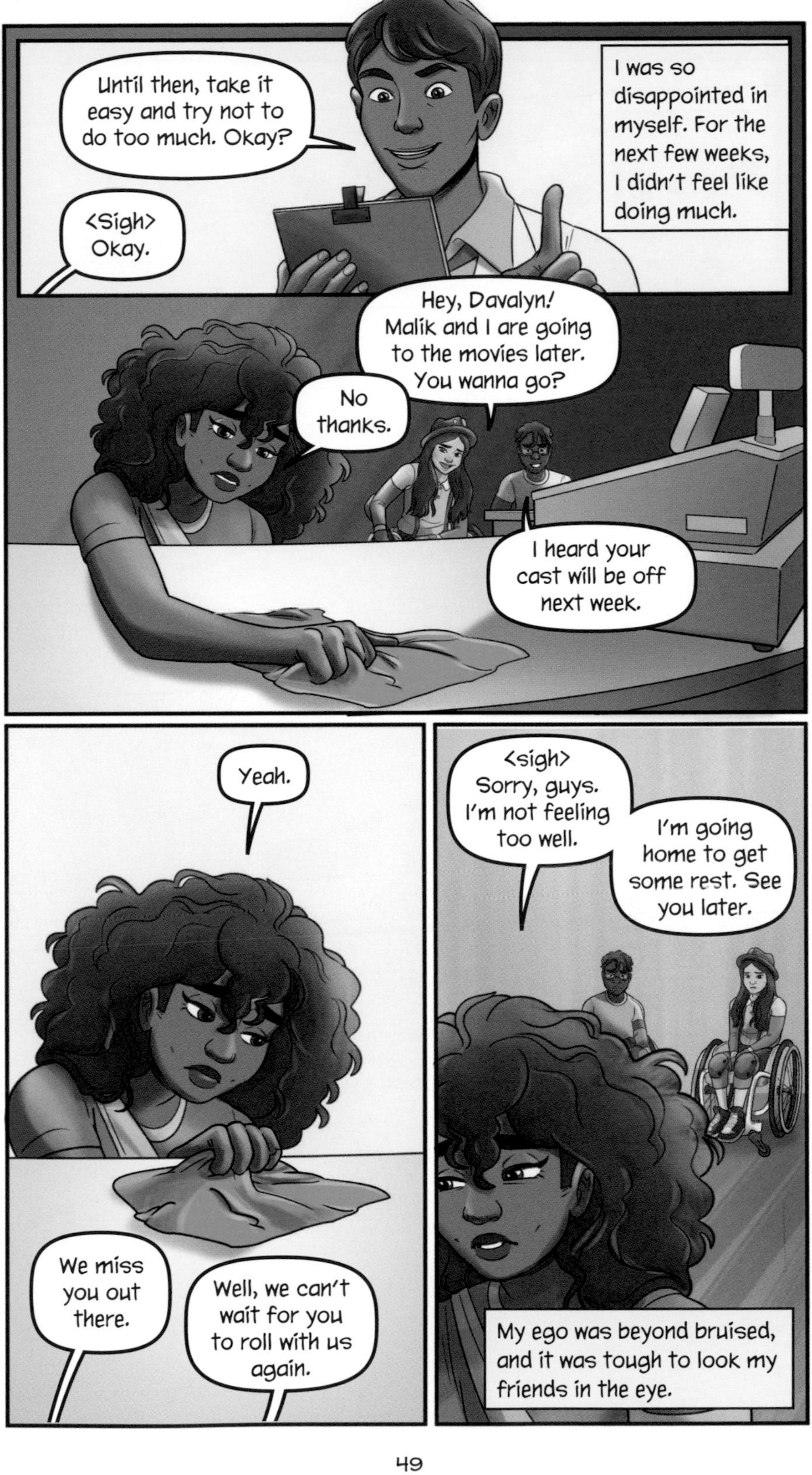
I was so disappointed in myself. For the next few weeks, I didn't feel like doing much.
Until then, take it easy and try not to do too much. Okay?
<Sigh> Okay.
Hey, Davalyn! Malik and I are going to the movies later. You wanna go?
No thanks.
I heard your cast will be off next week.
Yeah.
We miss you out there.
Well, we can't wait for you to roll with us again.
<sigh> Sorry, guys. I'm not feeling too well.
I'm going home to get some rest. See you later.
My ego was beyond bruised, and it was tough to look my friends in the eye.

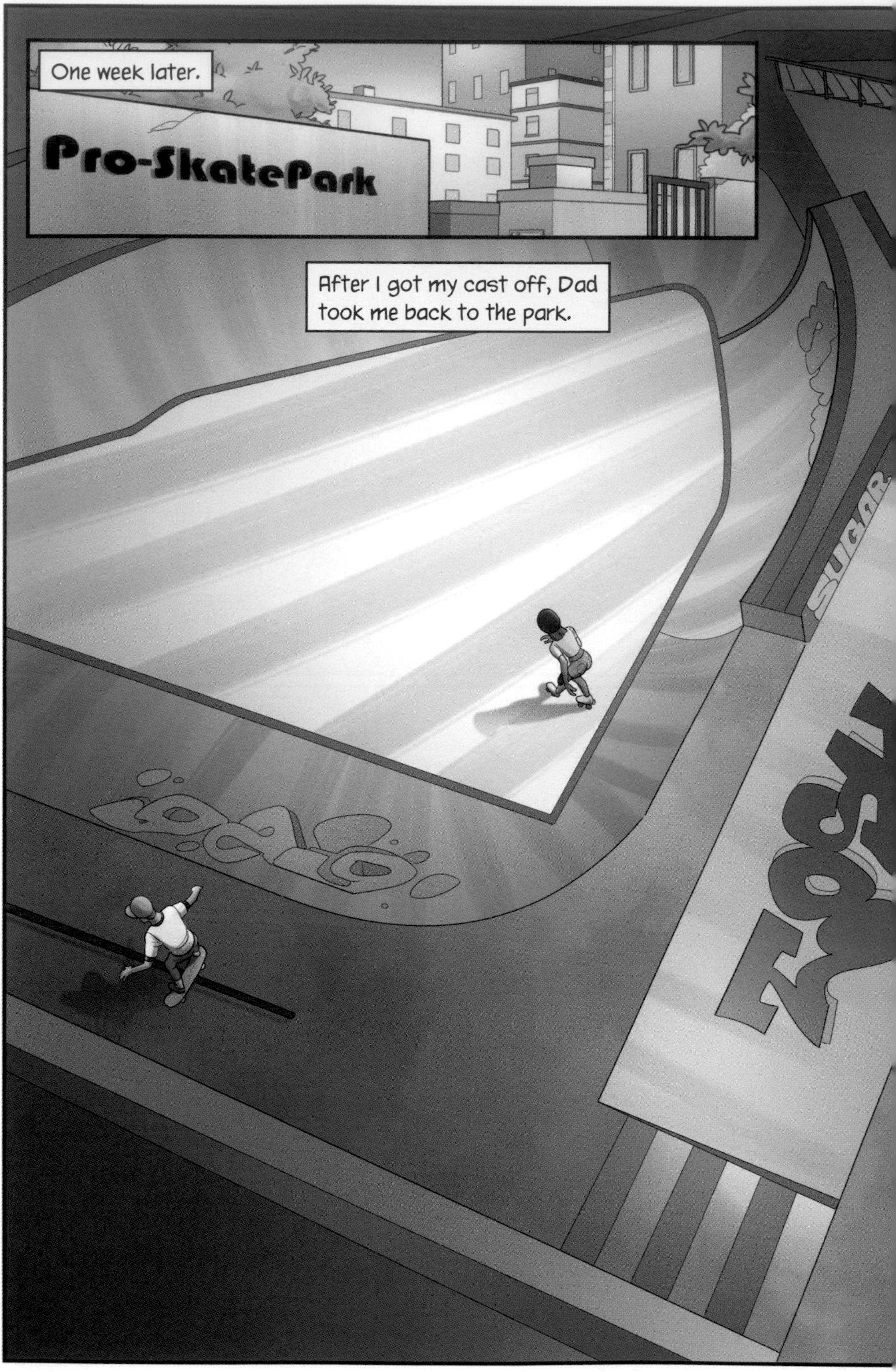
One week later.
Pro-SkatePark
After I got my cast off, Dad took me back to the park.
SUGAR

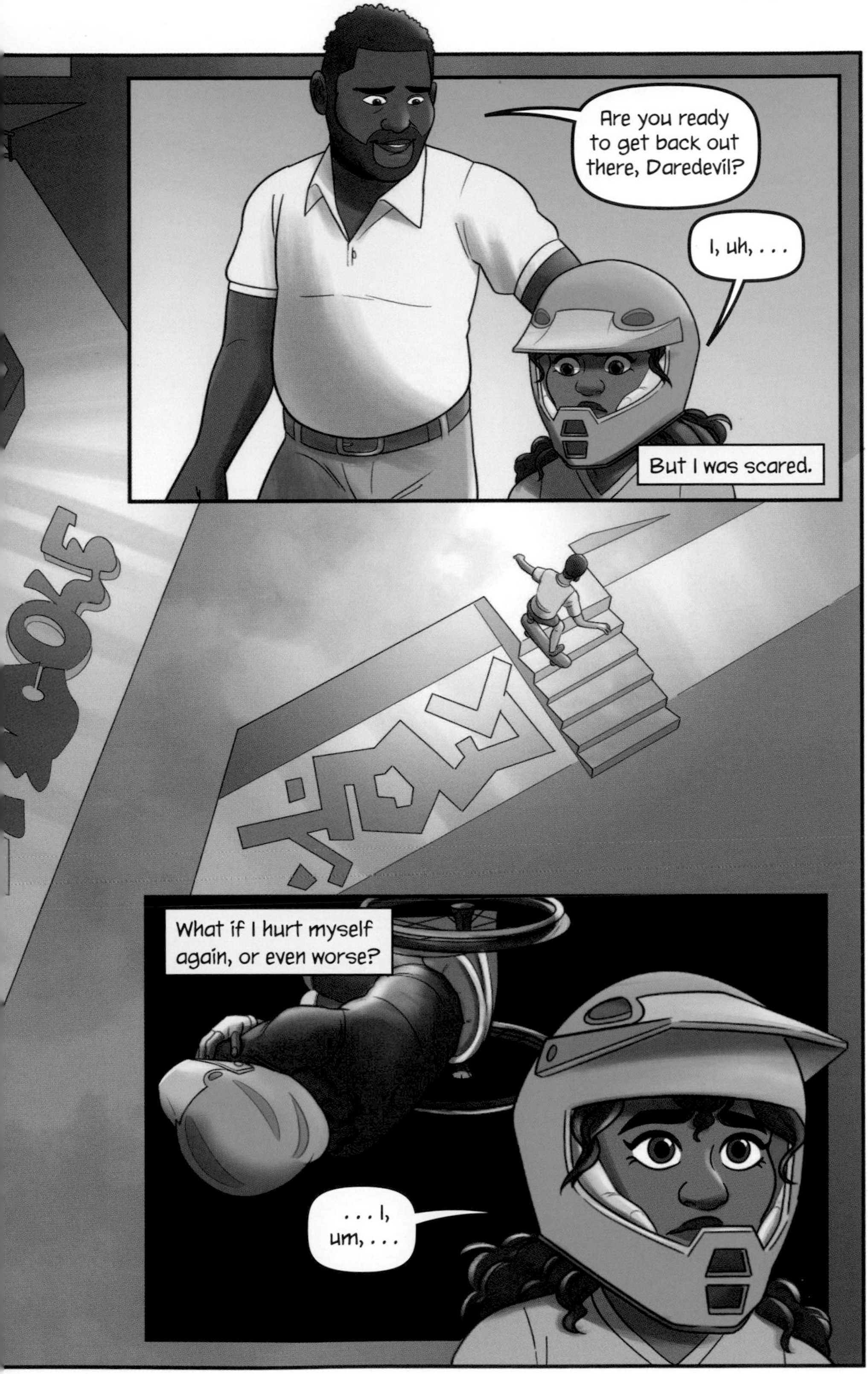
Are you ready to get back out there, Daredevil?
I, uh, . . .
But I was scared.
What if I hurt myself again, or even worse?
. . . I, um, . . .

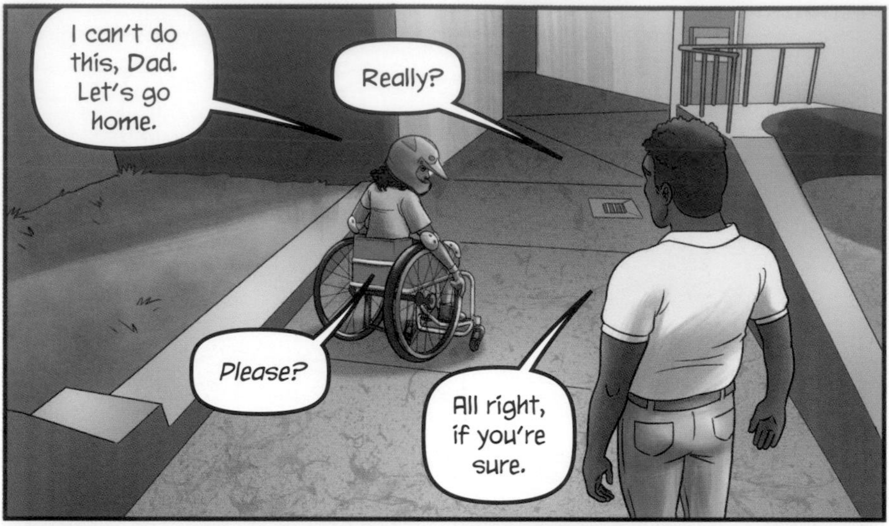
I can't do this, Dad. Let's go home.
Really?
Please?
All right, if you're sure.

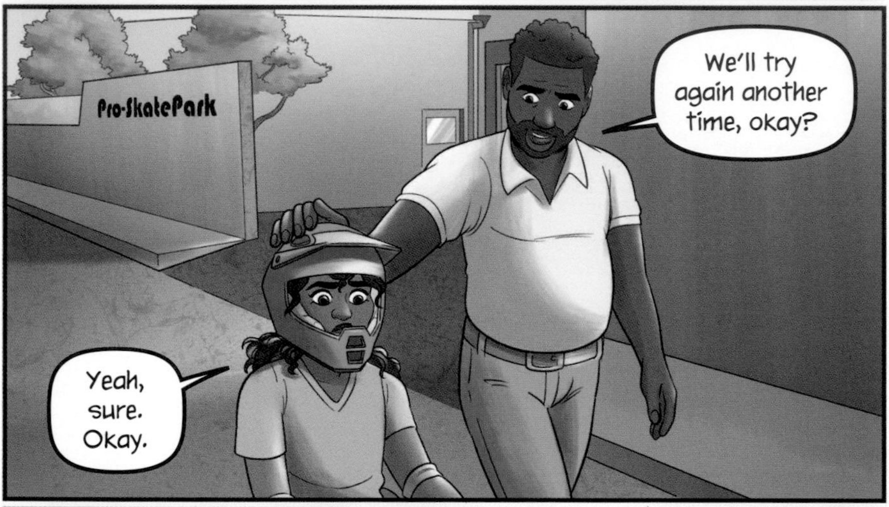
Pro-SkatePark
We'll try again another time, okay?
Yeah, sure. Okay.

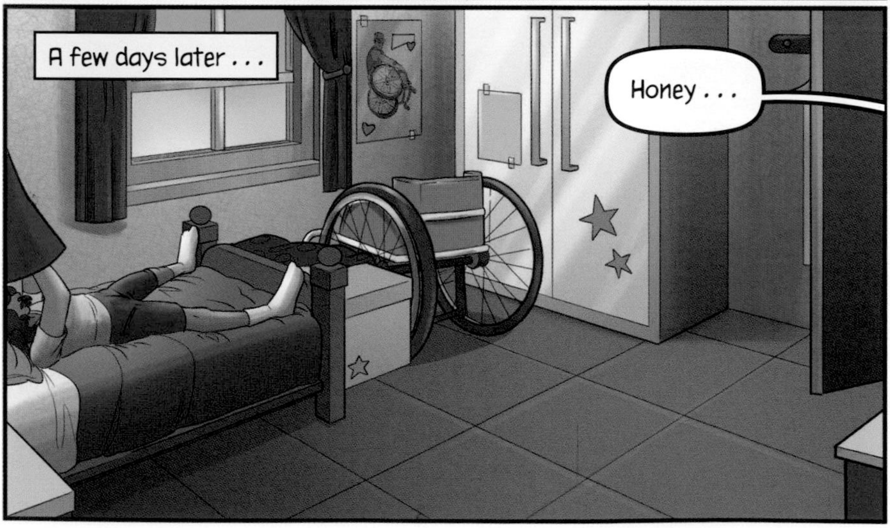
A few days later . . .
Honey . . .

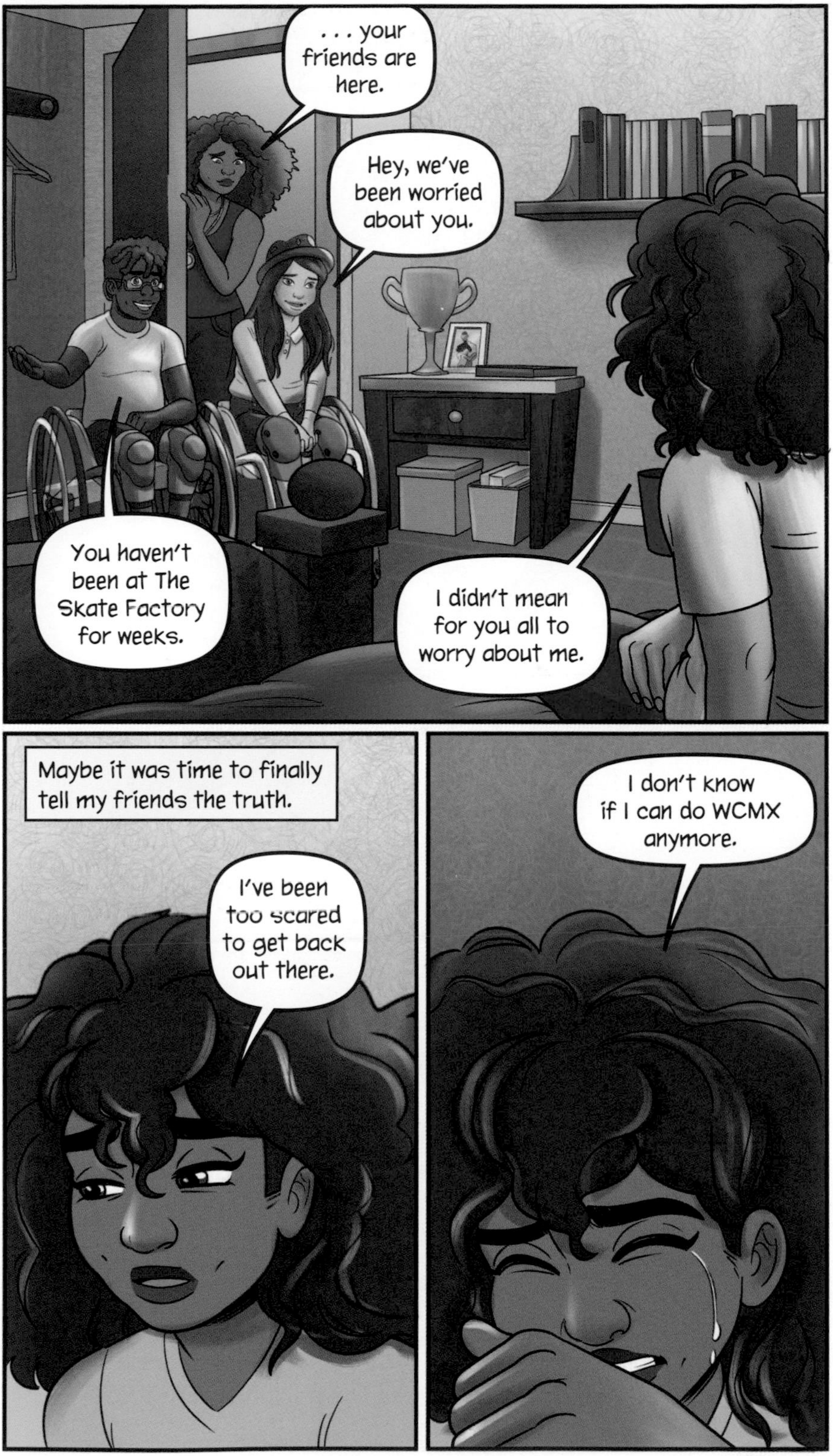
. . . your friends are here.
Hey, we've been worried about you.
You haven't been at The Skate Factory for weeks.
I didn't mean for you all to worry about me.
Maybe it was time to finally tell my friends the truth.
I've been too scared to get back out there.
I don't know if I can do WCMX anymore.

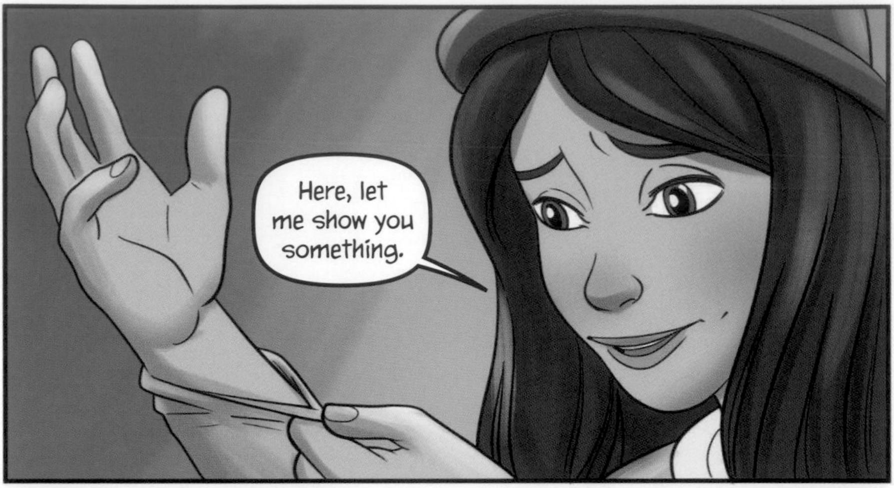
Here, let me show you something.

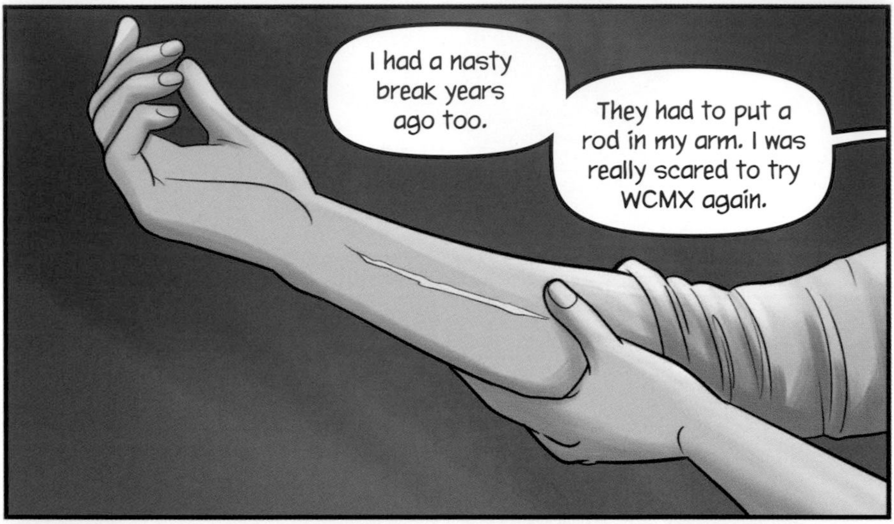
I had a nasty break years ago too.
They had to put a rod in my arm. I was really scared to try WCMX again.

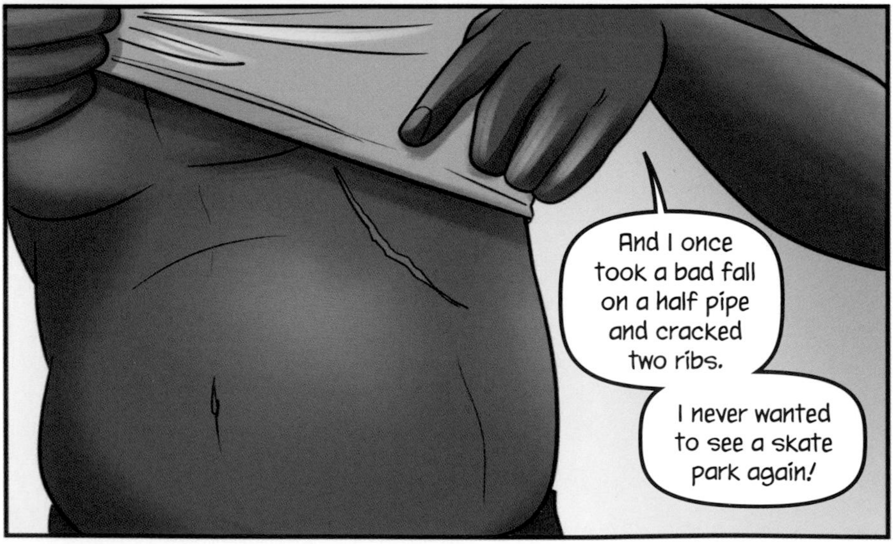
And I once took a bad fall on a half pipe and cracked two ribs.
I never wanted to see a skate park again!

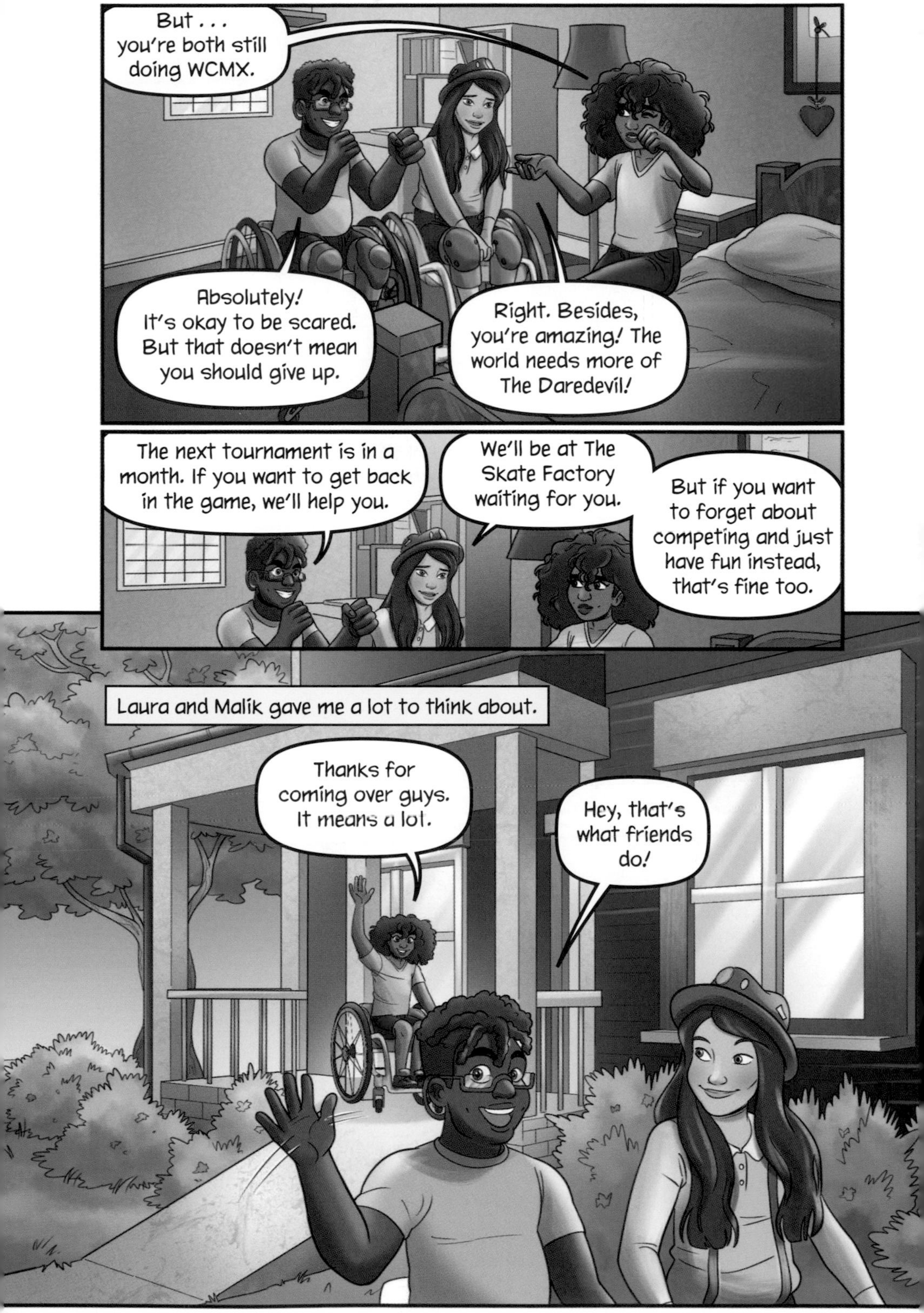
But . . . you're both still doing WCMX.
Absolutely! It's okay to be scared. But that doesn't mean you should give up.
Right. Besides, you're amazing! The world needs more of The Daredevil!
The next tournament is in a month. If you want to get back in the game, we'll help you.
We'll be at The Skate Factory waiting for you.
But if you want to forget about competing and just have fun instead, that's fine too.
Laura and Malik gave me a lot to think about.
Thanks for coming over guys. It means a lot.
Hey, that's what friends do!

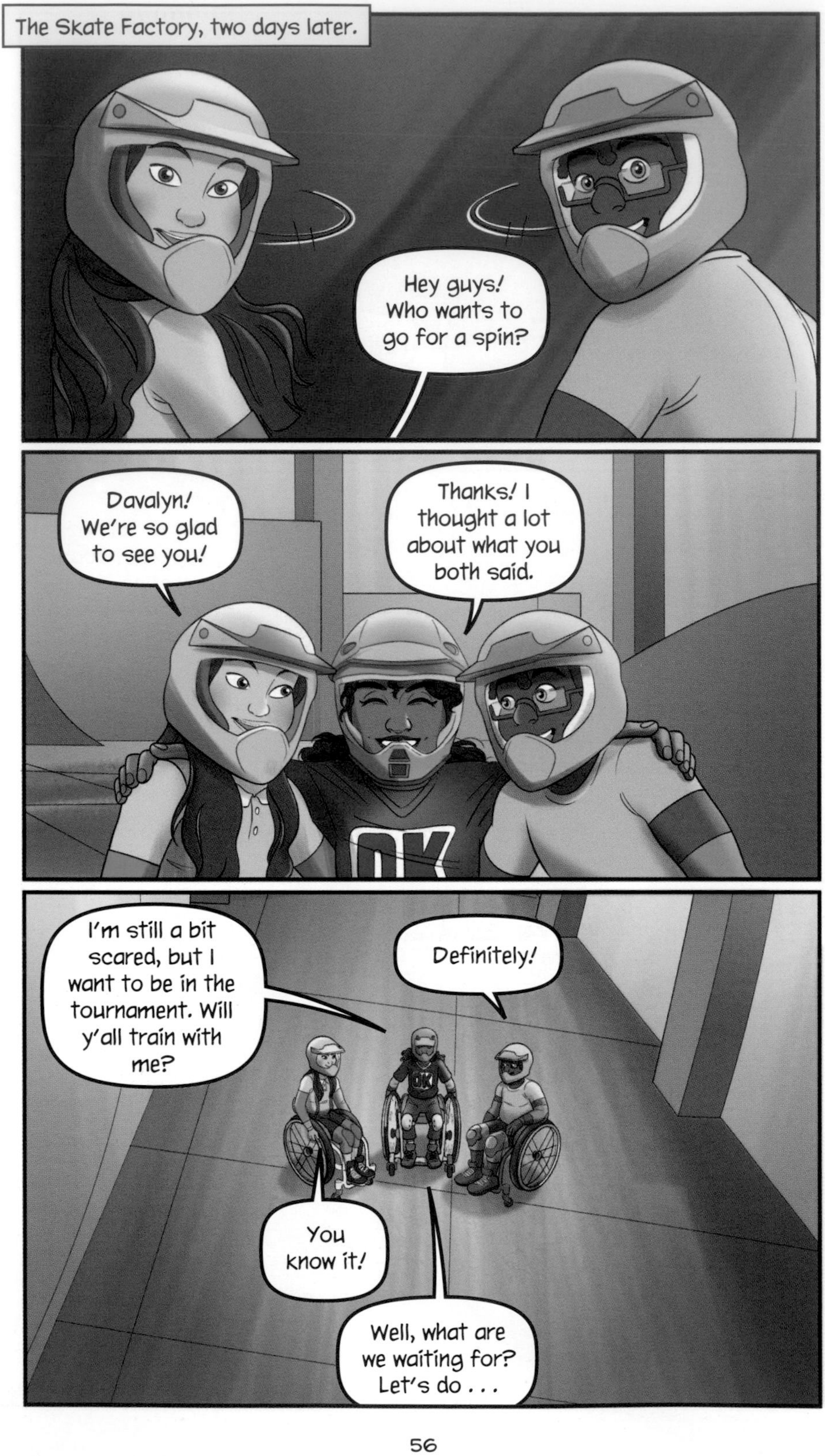
The Skate Factory, two days later.
Hey guys! Who wants to go for a spin?
Davalyn! We're so glad to see you!
Thanks! I thought a lot about what you both said.
I'm still a bit scared, but I want to be in the tournament. Will y'all train with me?
Definitely!
You know it!
Well, what are we waiting for? Let's do . . .

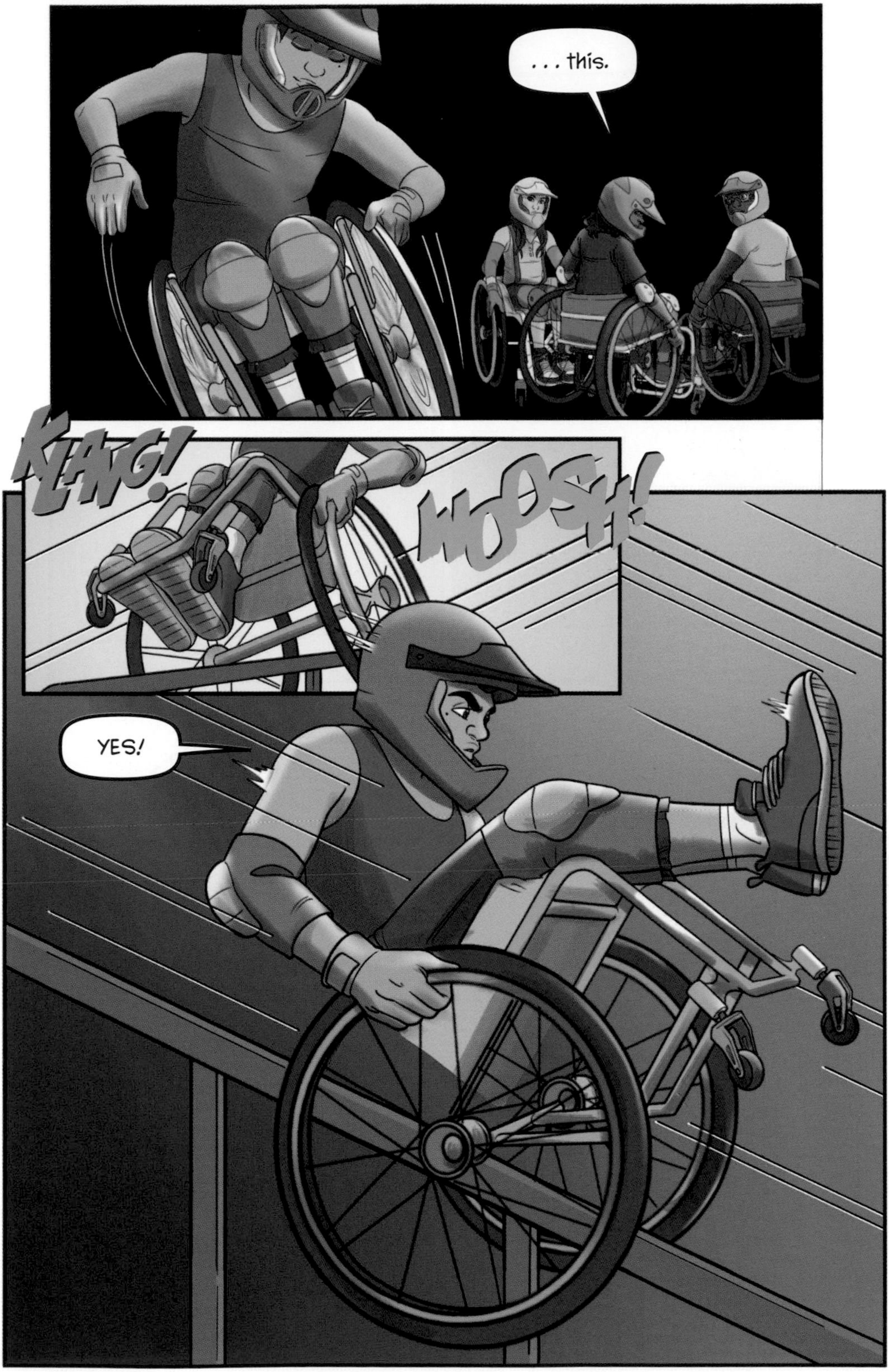
. . . this.
KLANG!
WOOSH!
YES!

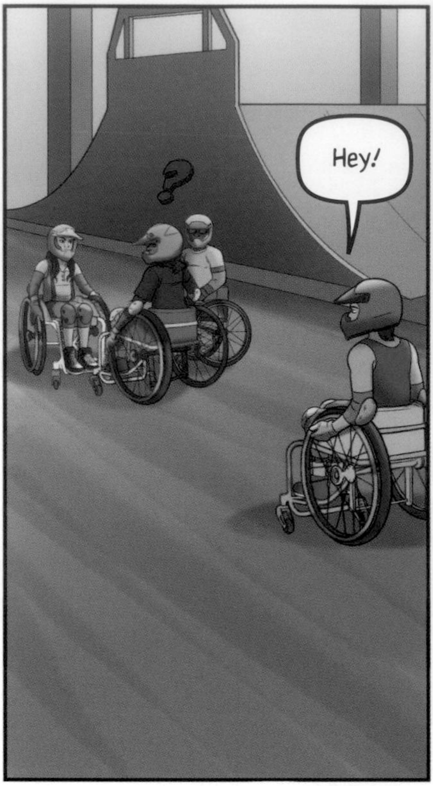
Hey!

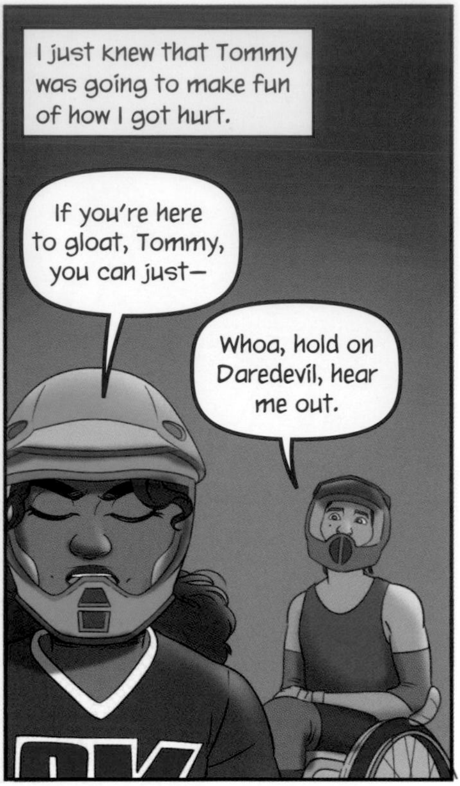
I just knew that Tommy was going to make fun of how I got hurt.
If you're here to gloat, Tommy, you can just—
Whoa, hold on Daredevil, hear me out.

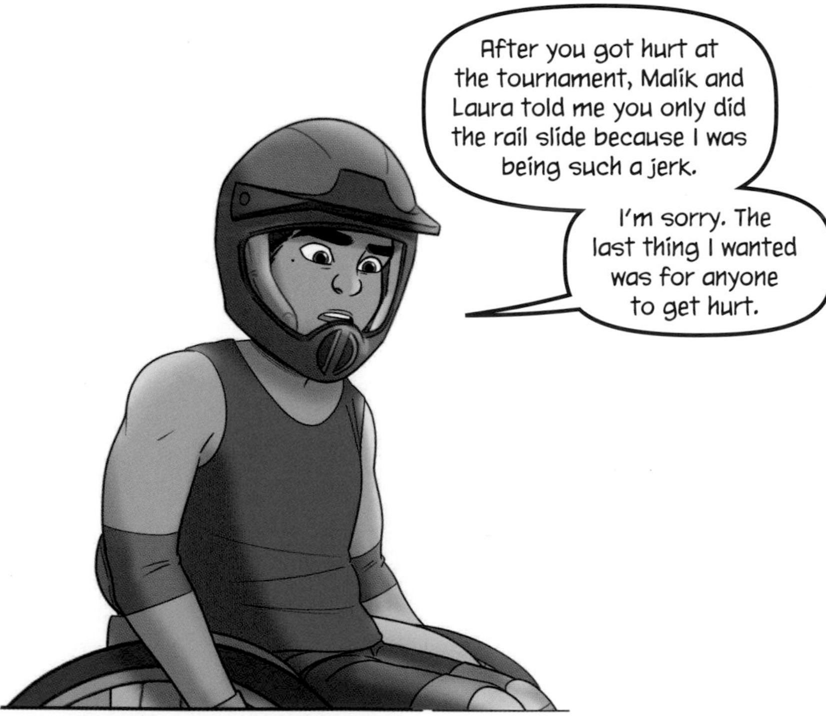
After you got hurt at the tournament, Malik and Laura told me you only did the rail slide because I was being such a jerk.
I'm sorry. The last thing I wanted was for anyone to get hurt.

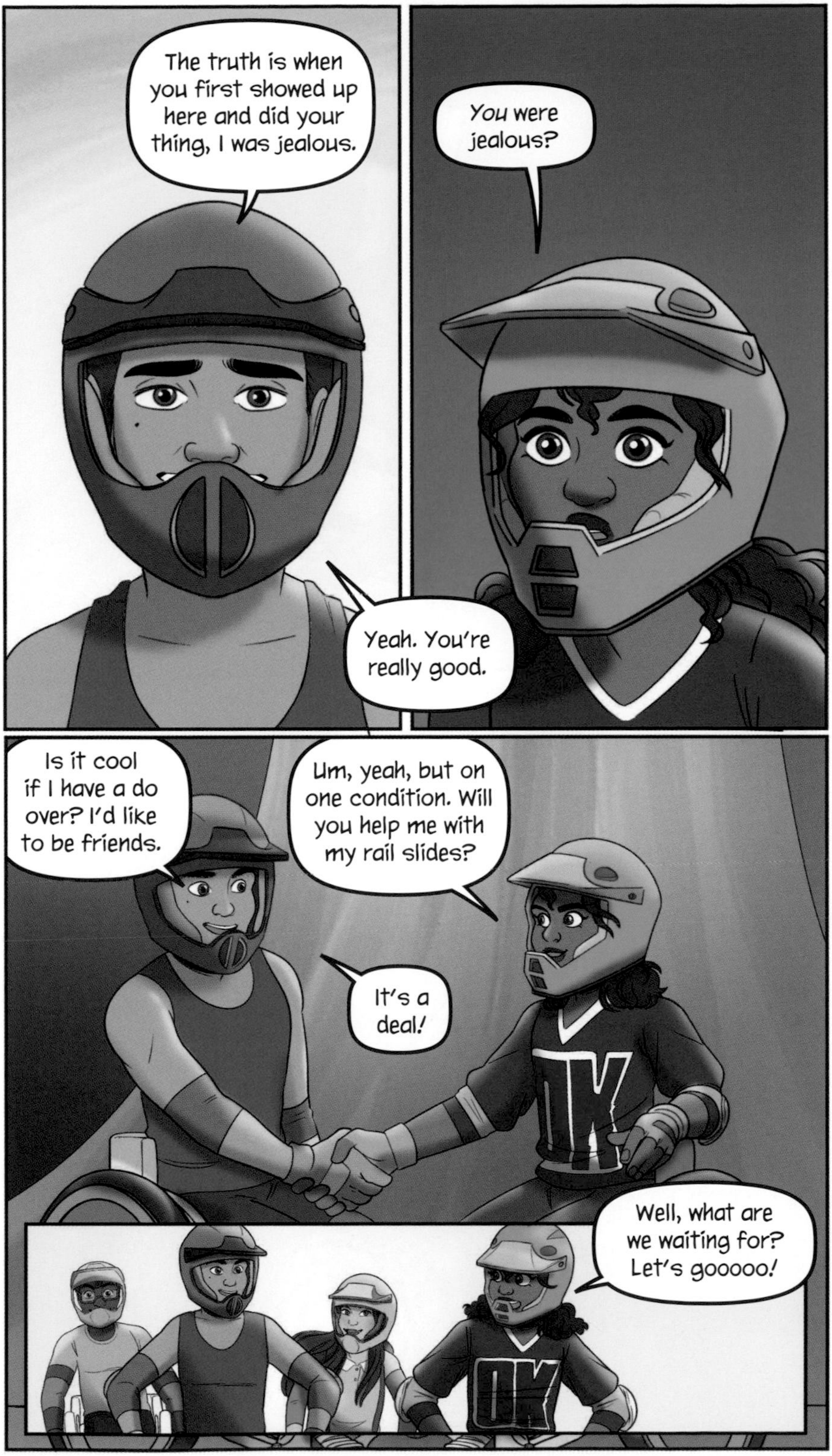
The truth is when you first showed up here and did your thing, I was jealous.
You were jealous?
Yeah. You're really good.
Is it cool if I have a do over? I'd like to be friends.
Um, yeah, but on one condition. Will you help me with my rail slides?
It's a deal!
Well, what are we waiting for? Let's gooooo!

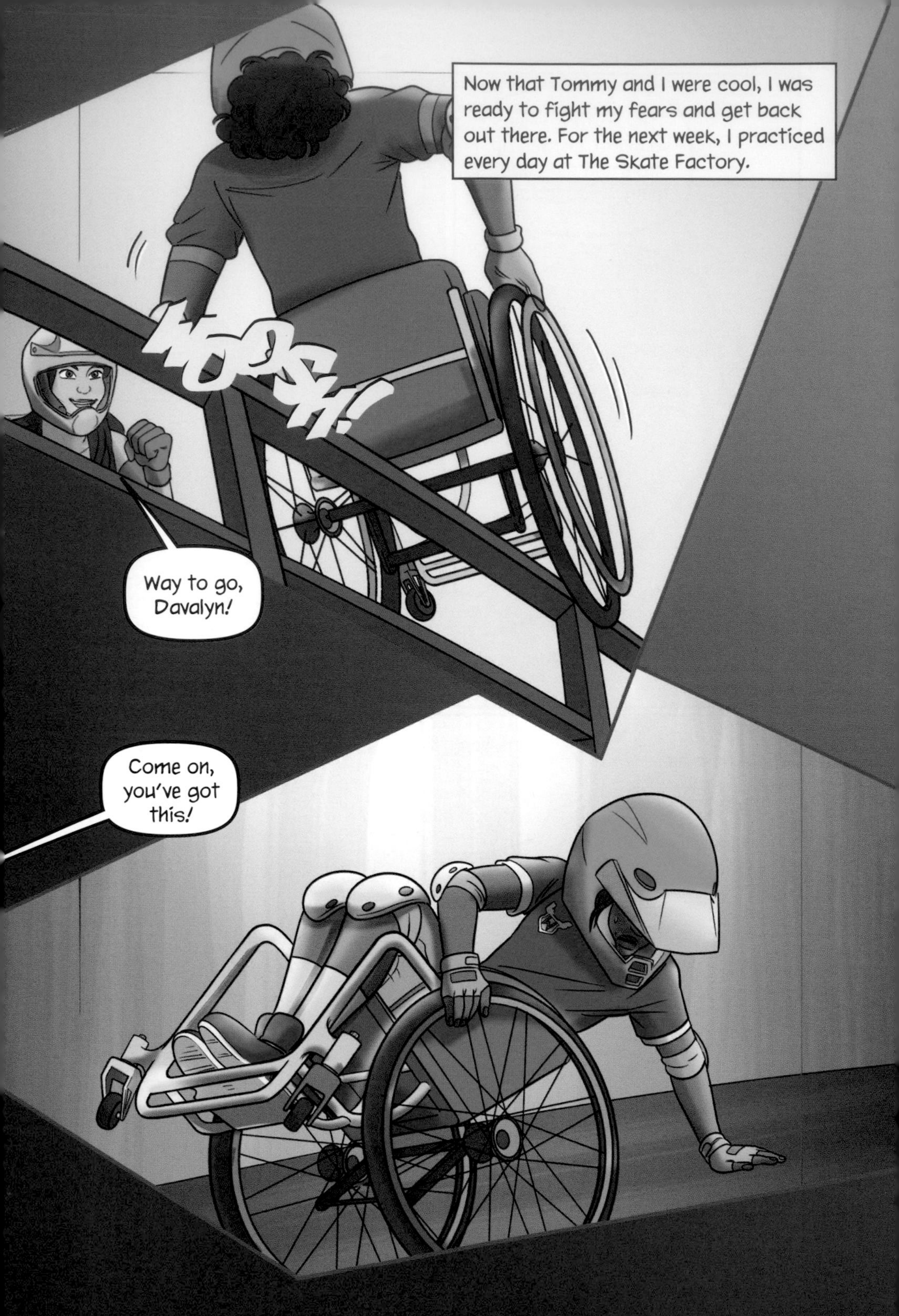
Now that Tommy and I were cool, I was ready to fight my fears and get back out there. For the next week, I practiced every day at The Skate Factory.
WOOSH!
Way to go, Davalyn!
Come on, you've got this!

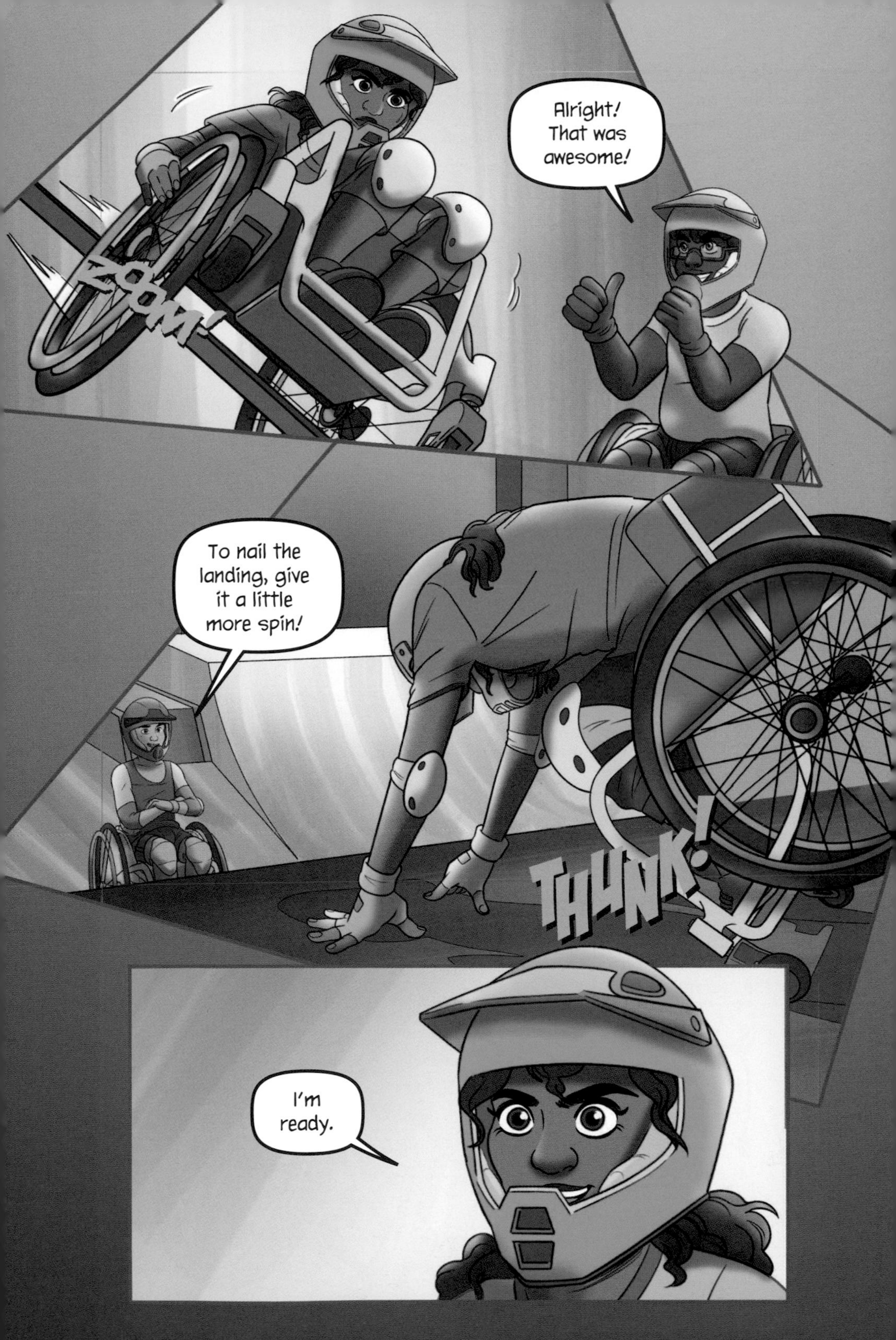
ZOOM!
Alright! That was awesome!
To nail the landing, give it a little more spin!
THUNK!
I'm ready.

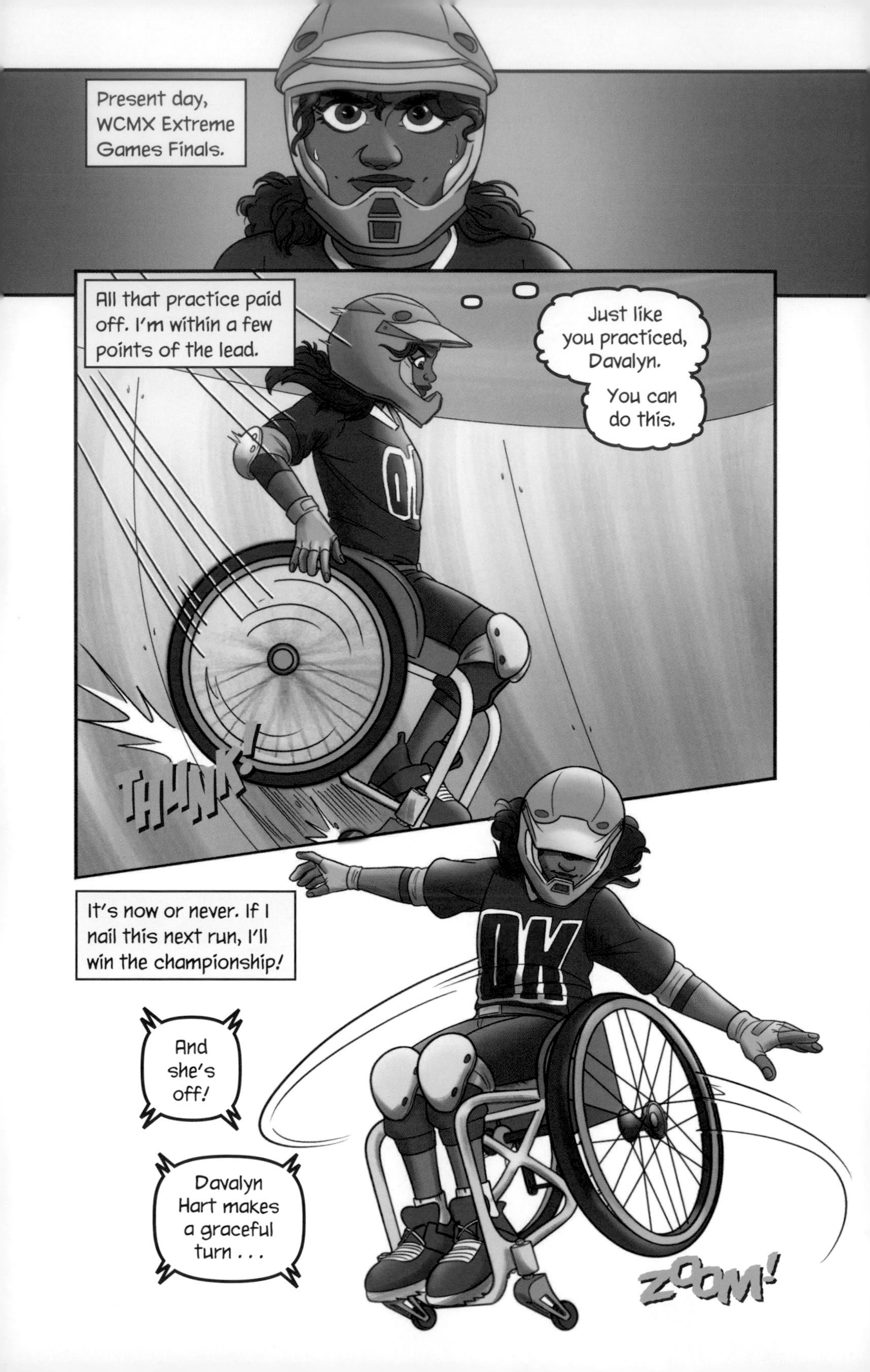
Present day, WCMX Extreme Games Finals.
All that practice paid off. I'm within a few points of the lead.
Just like you practiced, Davalyn.
You can do this.
THUNK!
It's now or never. If I nail this next run, I'll win the championship!
And she's off!
Davalyn Hart makes a graceful turn . . .
ZOOM!

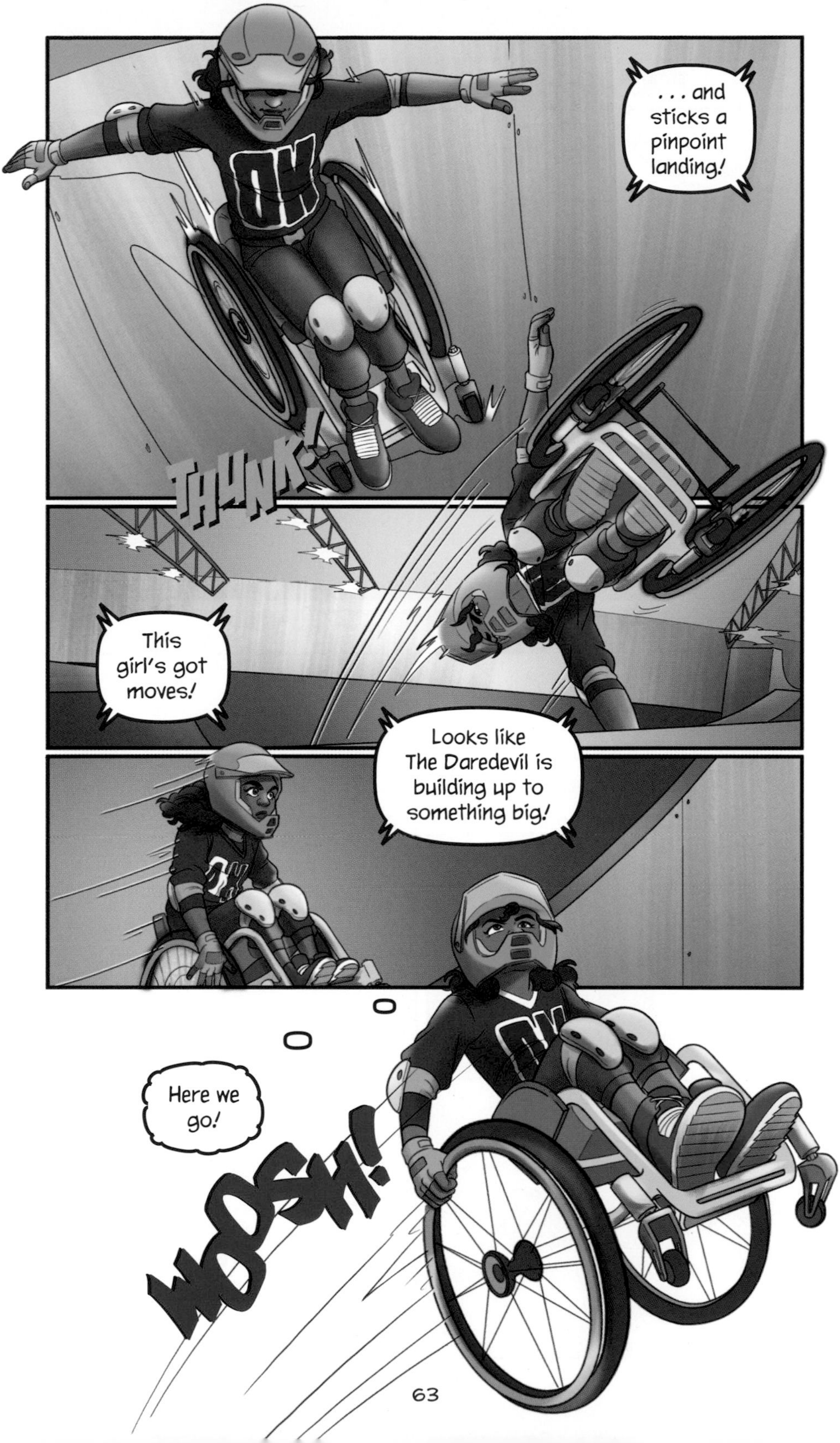
. . . and sticks a pinpoint landing!
THUNK!
This girl's got moves!
Looks like The Daredevil is building up to something big!
Here we go!
WOOSH!

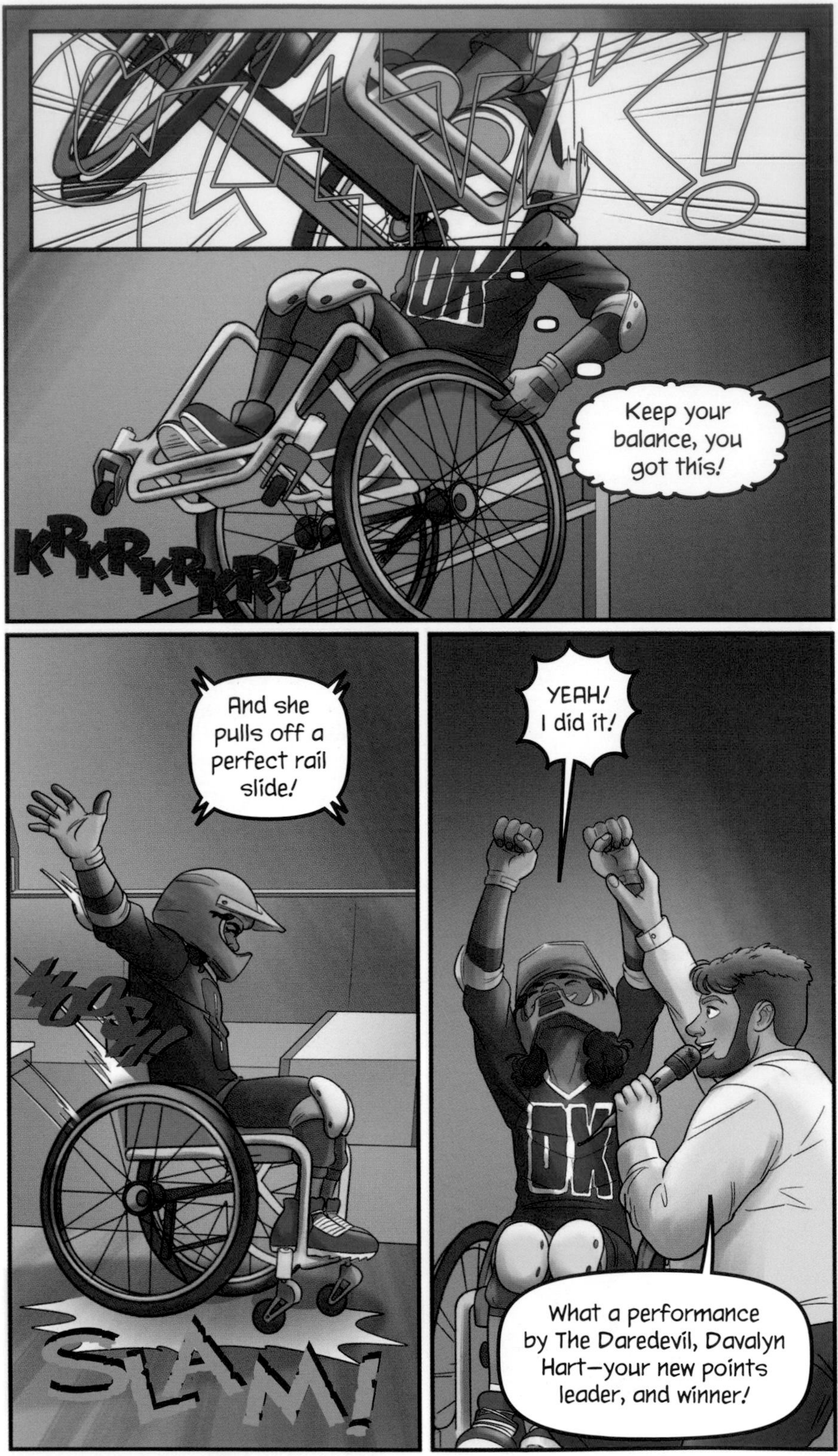

Keep your balance, you got this!
KRKRKRKR!
And she pulls off a perfect rail slide!
SLAM!
YEAH! I did it!
What a performance by The Daredevil, Davalyn Hart—your new points leader, and winner!

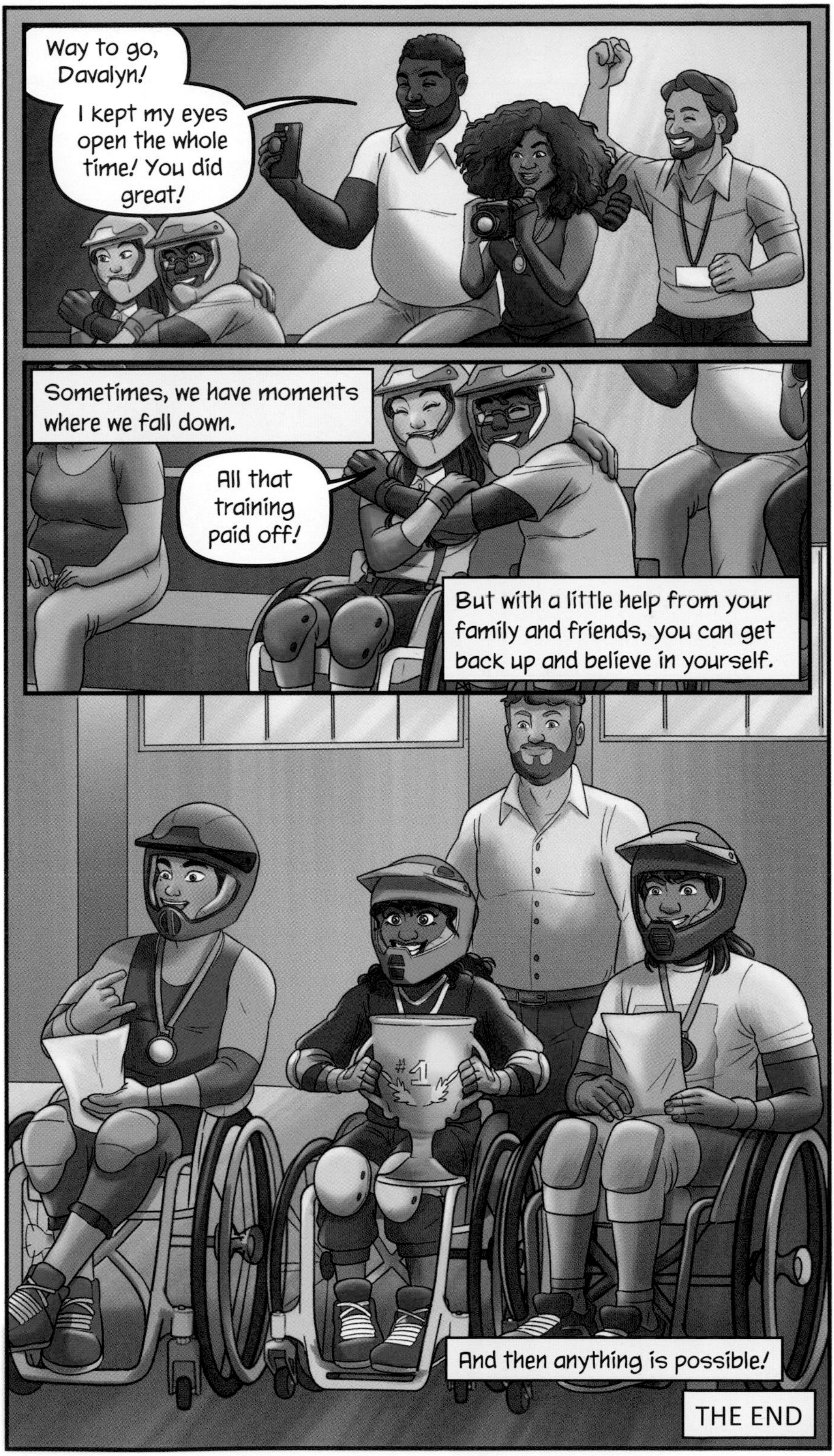
Way to go, Davalyn!
I kept my eyes open the whole time! You did great!
Sometimes, we have moments where we fall down.
All that training paid off!
But with a little help from your family and friends, you can get back up and believe in yourself.
#1
And then anything is possible!
THE END

VISUAL DISCUSSION QUESTIONS

1. Look at Davalyn's stunt in the panel to the right. What does this tell you about her? Does it show if she has any limitations? Can you tell what kind of skills she has and what she enjoys?

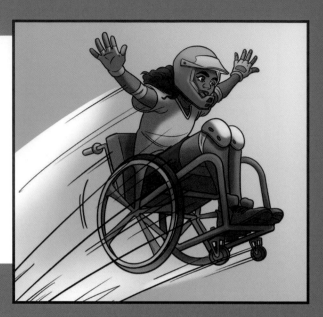

2. Silhouettes can help add a lot of drama to a scene and help you focus on a character's action. What feeling do you get from these images? How do they add to the story?

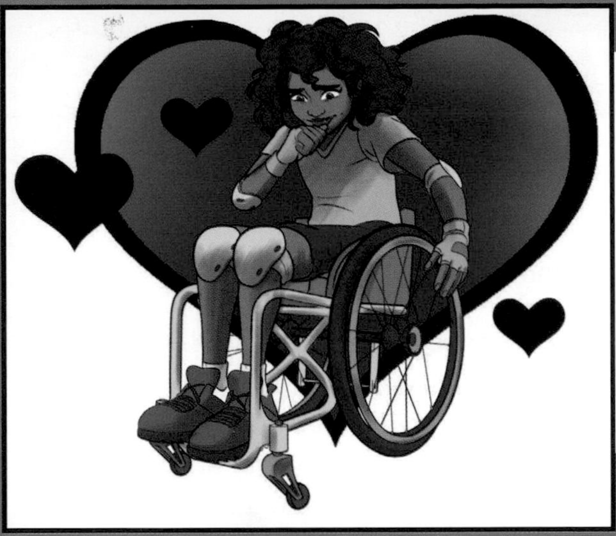

3. In graphic novels, the art can often show a character's emotions better than words. What do you think Davalyn is feeling in this scene?

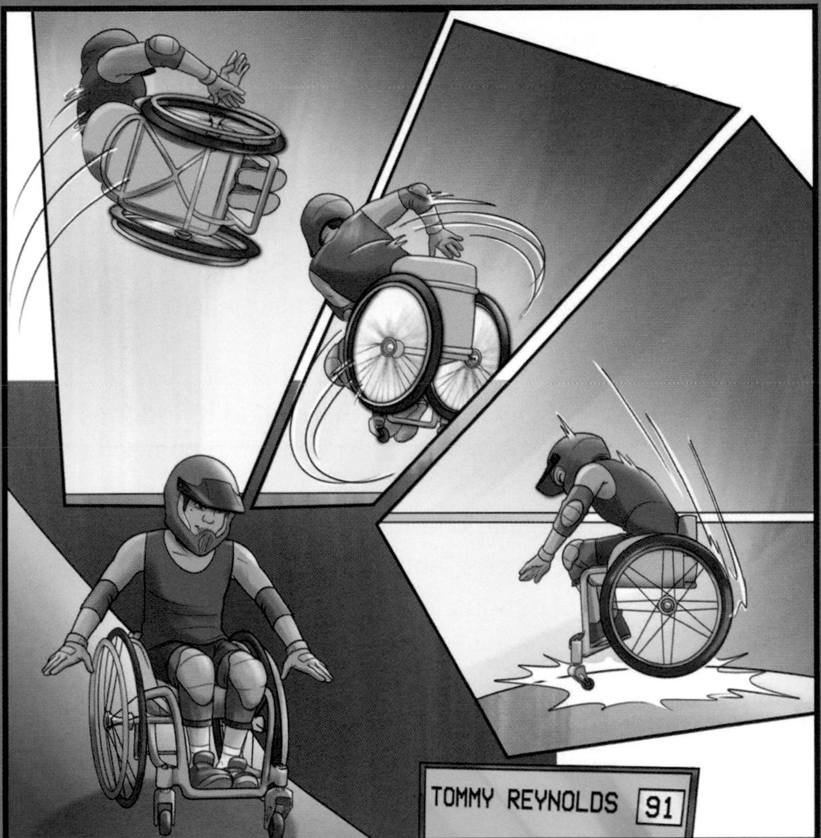
TOMMY REYNOLDS 91

4. Look at the sequence of panels above. Why do you think the artist chose to show the action this way? If you were drawing this stunt, would you show it in a different way?

FUN WHEELCHAIR MOTOCROSS FACTS

WCMX is an abbreviation for Wheelchair Motocross.

Aaron Fotheringham was diagnosed with a spinal cord defect at birth. But he didn't let that stop him. Also known as "Wheelz," Fotheringham created the sport of Wheelchair Motocross. Wheelz holds the current record for the farthest wheelchair ramp jump, clearing 70 feet (21 meters)!

Katherine Beattie is the first female WCMXer to land a wheelchair backflip.

Timothy Lachlan is the first Australian to land a wheelchair backflip.

Some WCMX Wheelchairs are custom-built. They're made out of titanium and are very lightweight. Some have small, skateboard-type wheels or even suspension systems that help riders do cool tricks!

In 2019, 15-year-old Lily Rice was the United Kingdom's first ever WCMX champion.

For difficult and sometimes dangerous tricks, WCMX riders wear helmets, neck braces, and other protective equipment to reduce the risk of serious injury.

The WCMX & Adaptive Skate World Championships started in 2016 and are held every year. The event showcases the best in Wheelchair Motocross and Adaptive Skating.

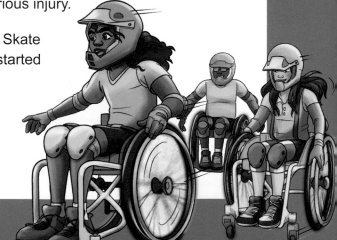

WHEELCHAIR MOTOCROSS TERMS

bank—a slanted or flat surface

coping—the round bar that surrounds the rim of skater pools and most ramps

deck—a flat landing that can be found on the top of quarter pipes and half pipes

flat rail—a straight metal bar used to do tricks like grinds and slides

half pipe—two quarter pipes on opposite sides of each other connected by a flat area between them

kicker—a small, often portable ramp used for launching into the air

mini ramp—a ramp that is usually 5 feet (1.5 meters) high or smaller

pyramid—a type of ramp that has four sides

quarter pipe—a lone, transitional ramp that is a quarter of a full pipe; it's a section that can be of any angle or size

roll—a large quarter pipe with no coping that is used to gain speed

vert—any transition piece on a skatepark that goes upwards and allows a skater to go up

volcano—a cylinder-style cone that has a flat or rounded top

GLOSSARY

axle (AK-suhl)—a rod attached to the center of the wheels on a wheelchair, cart, or vehicle; the wheels spin around the axle

caster wheel (KAS-ter weel)—a small wheel that swivels and allows a chair to turn easily

daredevil (DAIR-dev-uhl)—a person who is bold and often takes risks

ego (EE-goh)—a person's sense of self-esteem or self-image

gloat (GLOHT)—to speak highly of oneself in order to mock others

jealous (JEL-uhss)—the feeling of wanting something that someone else has

rotation (roh-TAY-shuhn)—the motion of an object around a central point

spina bifida (SPINE-uh BIF-i-duh)—a defect in which part of the spinal cord bulges through the spinal column, usually resulting in physical disability

sponsor (SPON-sur)—a person or company that gives money and equipment to an athlete or team to help them compete

tournament (TUR-nuh-muhnt)—a contest in which the winner has won the most games or scored the most points

ABOUT THE AUTHOR

 **SHAWN PRYOR'S** (he/him) work includes the middle-grade graphic novel series Cash and Carrie (Action Lab Entertainment), the 2019 Glyph Nominated sports graphic novel Force (Action Lab Entertainment), several books for Capstone's Jake Maddox Sports and Adventure series, and the Kids Sports Stories series. In his free time, Shawn enjoys reading, cooking, listening to streaming music playlists, and talking about why Zack from the Mighty Morphin Power Rangers is the greatest superhero of all-time.

ABOUT THE ARTISTS

Erika Vitrano, born in Messina, Italy, Erika studied at the "School of Comics" in Palermo. In 2018 she won the contest "Tutti pazzi per il Fumetto," and came in second nationally. In 2020 she published her first comic book in Italy, *De Bello Philosophorum* for Ex Libris Editions. The same year, she worked with Capstone to illustrate *Home Plate Heist,* and as a colorist on the comic *Il Grande Blek*. She continues her career as a freelance artist.

Tiziana Musmeci is an illustrator and graphic designer from Italy. She is the author of the children's book trilogy "Red." She also worked as background artist for the cartoon *Alpacarl the Alpacop*, and as a colorist and illustrator for several comics and books. She loves nature and animation movies.

Jaymes Reed has operated the company Digital-CAPS: Comic Book Lettering since 2003. He has done lettering for many publishers, most notably Avatar Press. He's also the only letterer working with Inception Strategies, an Aboriginal-Australian publisher that develops social comics with public service messages for the Australian government. Jaymes is a 2012 and 2013 Shel Dorf Award Nominee.

READ THEM ALL!

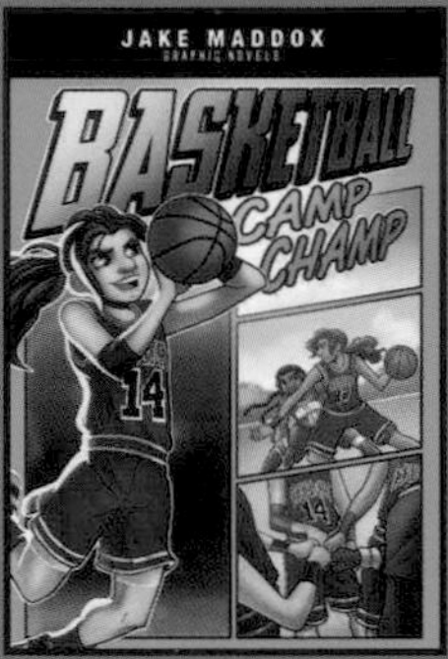
JAKE MADDOX
GRAPHIC NOVELS
BASKETBALL CAMP CHAMP

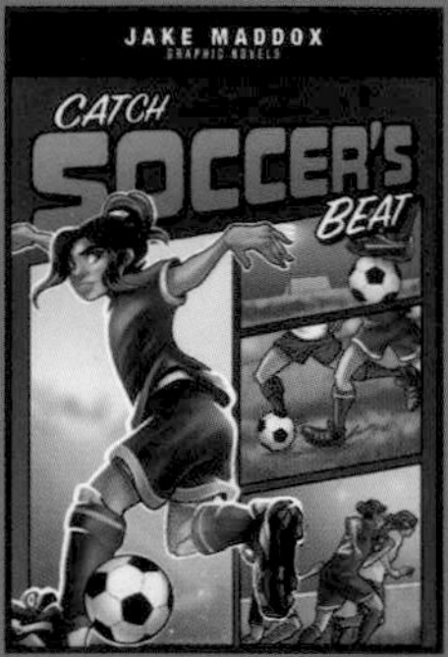
JAKE MADDOX
GRAPHIC NOVELS
CATCH SOCCER'S BEAT

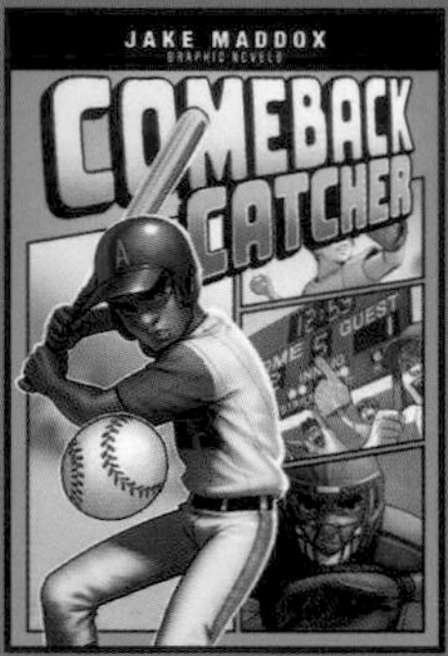
JAKE MADDOX
GRAPHIC NOVELS
COMEBACK CATCHER

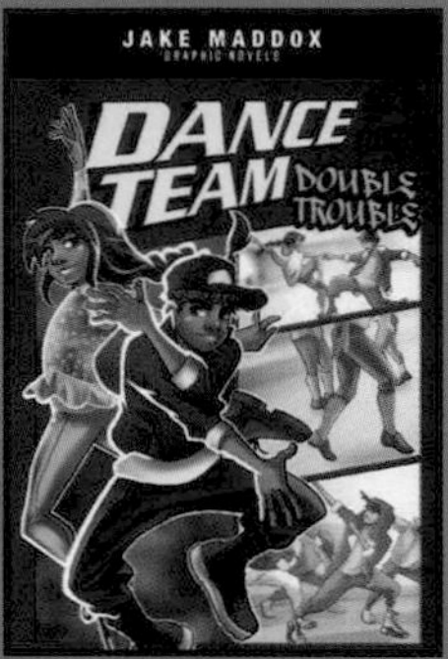
JAKE MADDOX
GRAPHIC NOVELS
DANCE TEAM DOUBLE TROUBLE

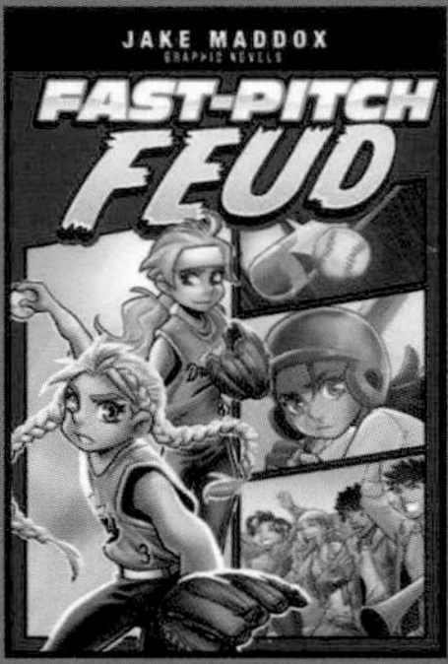
JAKE MADDOX
GRAPHIC NOVELS
FAST-PITCH FEUD

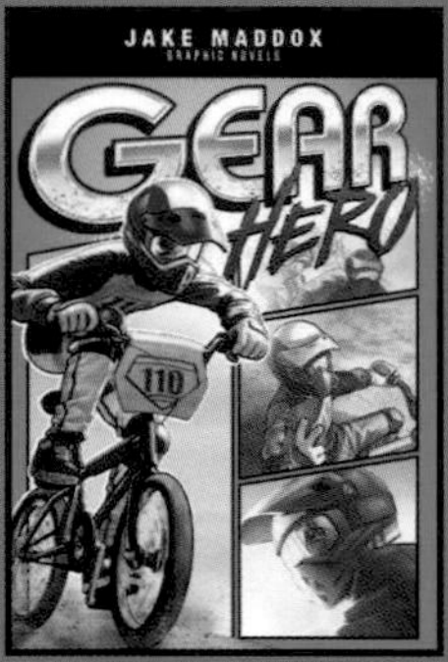
JAKE MADDOX
GRAPHIC NOVELS
GEAR HERO

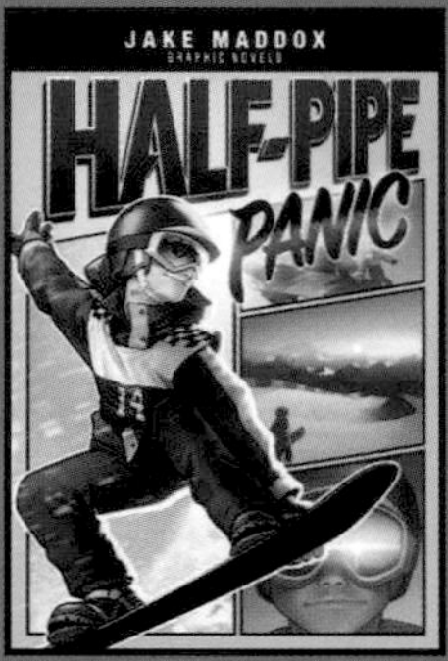
JAKE MADDOX
GRAPHIC NOVELS
HALF-PIPE PANIC

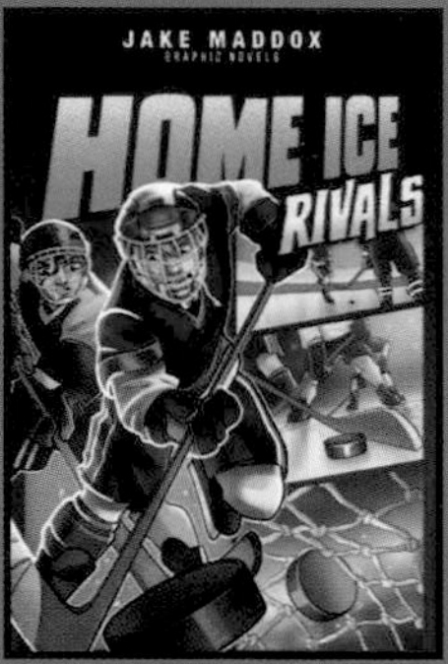
JAKE MADDOX
GRAPHIC NOVELS
HOME ICE RIVALS

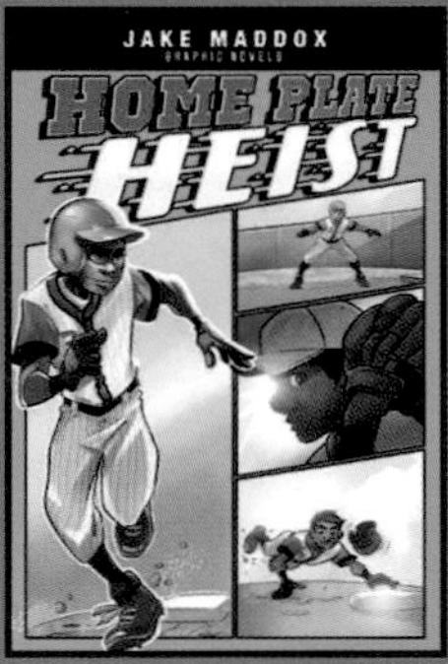
JAKE MADDOX
GRAPHIC NOVELS
HOME PLATE HEIST

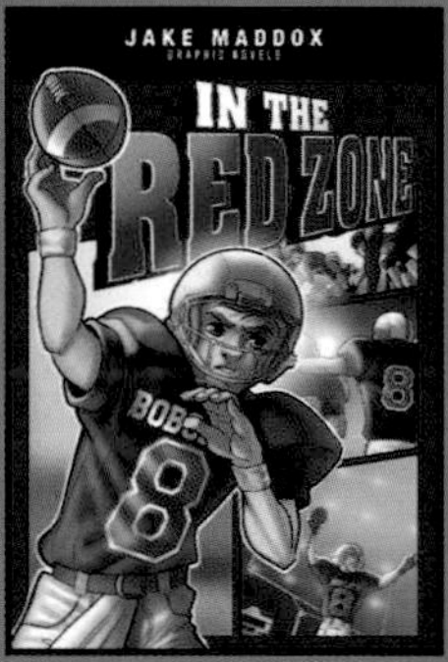
JAKE MADDOX
GRAPHIC NOVELS
IN THE RED ZONE

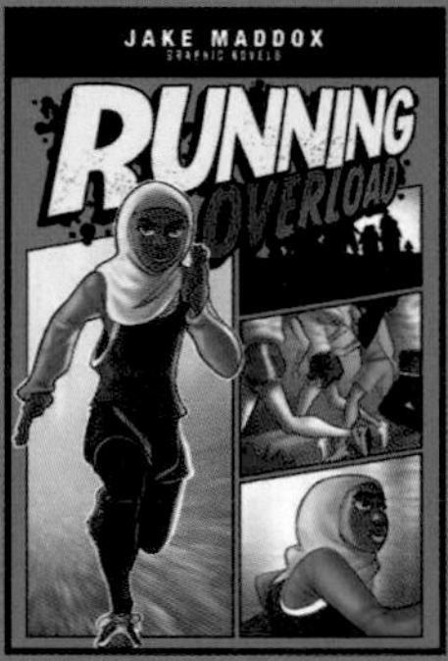
JAKE MADDOX
GRAPHIC NOVELS
RUNNING OVERLOAD

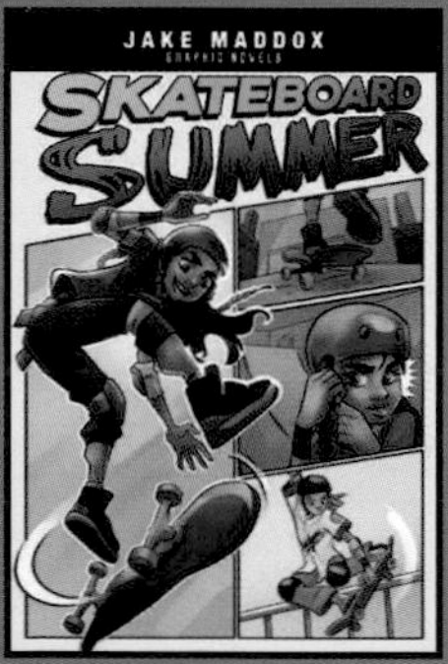
JAKE MADDOX
GRAPHIC NOVELS
SKATEBOARD SUMMER

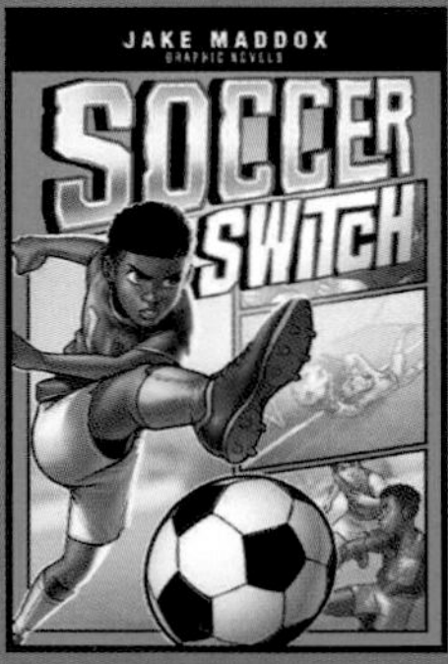
JAKE MADDOX
GRAPHIC NOVELS
SOCCER SWITCH

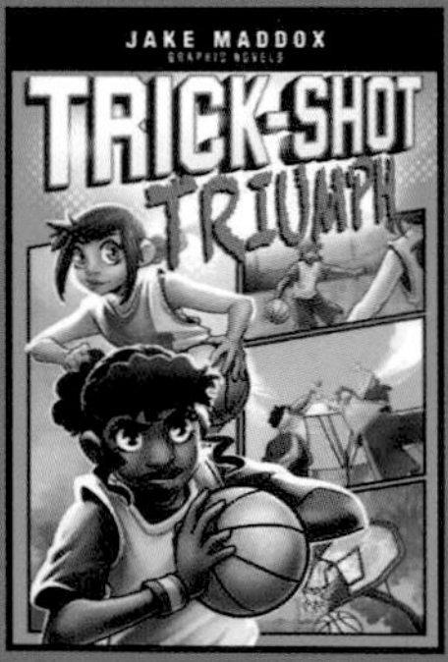
JAKE MADDOX
GRAPHIC NOVELS
TRICK-SHOT TRIUMPH

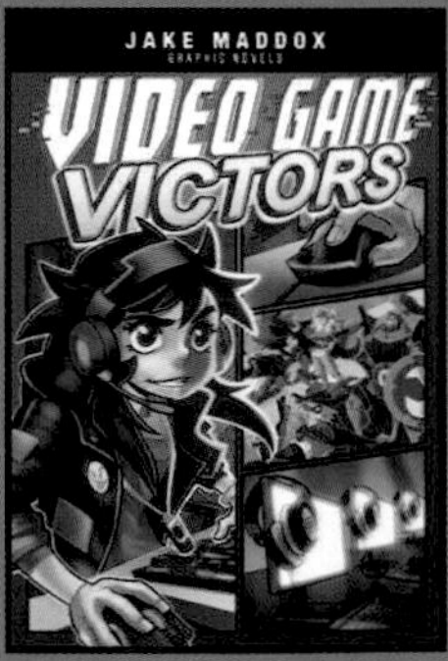
JAKE MADDOX
GRAPHIC NOVELS
VIDEO GAME VICTORS

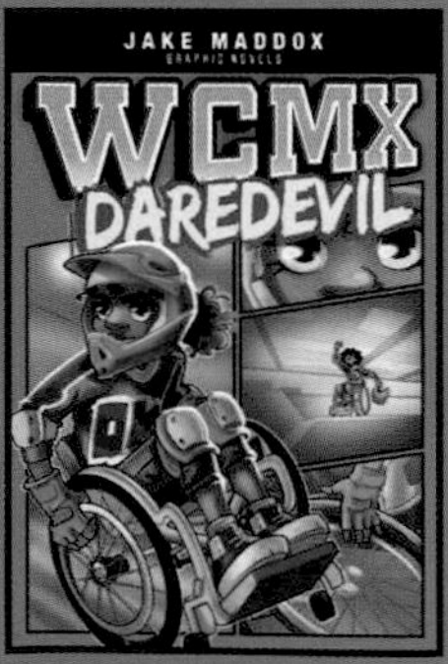
JAKE MADDOX
GRAPHIC NOVELS
WCMX DAREDEVIL